LOVE

BY

Delivery

SECOND EDITION

By
PAT SIMMONS

Cover: Tywebbins Creations
Copy editor: Chandra Sparks Splond
Proofreader: Judicious Revisions LLC

ISBN-13:978-1542602556
ISBN-10: 1542602556

PRAISES FOR PAT SIMMONS

"I believe that this is Pat's greatest novel, but I say that about all of her books. LOL. *Love Led by the Spirit* is captivating. Pat had me hooked from page two until the end of the book. Every time I tried to put it down, the next chapter would pull me in."—Ceisha Lee on *Love led by the Spirit*

"So great I could not stop reading until I finished it. Bought it and started reading at 6 p.m., finished by 8 p.m., writing the review at 8:30 p.m. Pat Simmons is one of my favorite authors, and this book clearly shows why. It reminds you that no matter what you are dealing with, God is the solution to every problem, issue, and circumstance."—Joyce on *Every Woman Needs a Praying Man*

"*Couple By Christmas* is a beautiful story of love, faith, and reconciliation. I always love reading books by this great author Pat Simmons because she always lets God guide the pen to create wonderful stories with well-developed characters to minister to the readers through the story."—Milton Kelley

"I am just beyond happy. Pat Simmons is truly amazing. I have read all her books, and I have been waiting for this one. Sandra finally got her Boaz. What sets Pat Simmons apart from others authors is her books *always* have a message for your spirit, healings for your mind, scriptures, history, plan of salvation, love. I not only enjoyed a beautiful novel, but I learn so much about our history."—Amazon reader on *The Confession*

Chapter 1

Still single. I've got the condo, the car, and the salary, so where is my husband?

It wasn't the first time Dominique Hayes' mind wandered as she attended the Friday night singles meeting. Of all the auxiliaries at Salvation Temple, she tried not to miss this weekly ministry—well, not anymore. Yet, as she shifted in her seat, Dominique wanted to wave a white clearance sign with bold red letters: AVAILABLE FOR DINNER, MOVIES, OR A WALK IN THE PARK. PICK ME.

How pathetic. She sounded like a stray puppy in a shelter, whining for a good home instead of a driven senior account manager. Since she was a teenager, she had trusted God for every blessing in her life: great position—almost six figures; home—spacious condo in a nice neighborhood; and good health.

Now, at thirty-three, she struggled with trusting the same Lord for finding her a mate, one of the opposite sex—of course she had to clarify today in this time of wickedness. But she didn't have to tell God that. He was the Creator of the guidelines for husbands and wives.

Two nice-looking men—tall, built, and meticulously groomed—strolled into the small sanctuary. They scanned the chapel. Dominique perked up, but slumped when Sisters Carr and McAllister waved and the gentlemen headed their direction.

"One day," Paige Blake, who was like the sister Dominique never had, whispered sitting next to her.

Dominique nodded, but didn't believe it. No one, besides her best friend knew she had been outside the safety net of Jesus and frequented a few clubs with associates in hopes of finding her special someone. The men wanted her body, and she wanted them in the Body of Christ.

In an effort to justify her dating the unsaved bachelors, she had invited Tyrone Kennedy to her church. After him was Sam Glover, and lastly, Jeff McCoy. None of them ever returned after one visit. Her mother, Dora, always said, "You can bring a horse to the water, but you can't make him drink." True, so Dominique repented and returned to the singles meeting with a new commitment to wait on God.

"Be prayerful, hopeful, and faithful," Minster Quinton Ray, their leader, advised the group. "God will show you the man or woman who's perfect for you."

Dominique guessed he was speaking from experience since he was recently engaged to a fairly new member. Of all the church ladies who had vied for the hunk's attention for months, in walked Mya King and the minister was a goner.

"I'm losing the hopeful part." Paige took the words right out of her mouth.

"I've lost my faith on this one too." Dominique sighed. Her expression had to mirror Paige's. "But we still have prayer," she said, trying to encourage them both.

"Amen," a sister in the pew behind them leaned over their shoulders, evidently eavesdropping.

Tonight the audience was smaller than the fifty-plus regulars. The numbers fluctuated, depending on if someone snagged a date, announced an engagement, or became discouraged and stopped attending as Dominique had once done.

Don't stop praying, God whispered in her ear.

She knew the Scripture the Lord referenced. Philippians 4:6: *Be careful for nothing; but in everything by prayer and supplication with thanksgiving let your requests be made known unto God.* She had been praying three years and nothing.

The minister challenged her mind to focus. "This month, we're fellowshipping at Strike-n-Spare with the single saints from Corinthian Church."

While some clapped, Dominique couldn't remember the last time she'd rolled a ball and hit more than three pins. The things she had to do to be on a female auction block. "You going?" she asked Paige.

"I plan to be the cutest bowler there, even if I

can't bowl."

It didn't take much effort for her friend to accomplish that. Her seductive hazel eyes were Paige's best feature while Dominique had the curves. Best friends since high school, they connected. They were often mistaken for sisters, but to them, they looked nothing alike. Dominique was fair skinned, petite at five-three, and preferred short hair. Paige's skin tone was a shade darker, and she had beautiful long, wavy hair. She beat Dominique's height by three inches.

"I guess I won't get my manicure that week." Dominique believed in staying on top of her beauty regimen, just in case she crossed paths with her soul mate.

After Minister Ray's pep talk, they sang inspiring worship songs and mingled with the same singles while enjoying light refreshments. Afterward, she and Paige parted ways for home. Even if Dominique did have a date, she was too exhausted to enjoy it. She'd had a crazy week at work, helping two of her managers under her score major accounts.

Before retiring to bed, she cried out to the Lord, thanking Him for His goodness and repenting of her misguided thoughts.

"Lord, I'm serious about trusting You for the right man." A tear dropped from her eye as her heart twisted. It was easy to profess. She paused when she recalled her church's dismissal Scripture, Psalm 19:14: *Let the words of my mouth, and the meditation of my heart, be acceptable in thy sight, O LORD, my strength, and my redeemer.*

4

She sniffed. Taking a deep breath, she exhaled with renewed resolve. "Lord, tonight I vow that I won't go out with another man who isn't in the Body of Christ. He has to have Your stamp of approval."

When you vow a vow unto Me, pay up! For I have no pleasure in fools. The Lord whispered Ecclesiastes 5:4 in her ear.

She trembled. Now that the solemn promise had spilled from her lips, she was reminded of the story in Judges 11. Unlike Jephthah's vow with a tragic end, Dominique prayed and hoped for a happy ending.

Driver Ashton Taylor had no complaints as he parked his company truck in front of the small bungalow on Rosedale Circle. The first day of spring had kept its promise of sunshine and an unseasonably warm breeze. Of course, the highlight of the week was he had a date that night. Well, sort of. His church's singles ministry would fellowship with a sister church at a bowling alley. The whole purpose of these excursions was for brothers to seek out a wife.

At thirty-seven, Ashton was ready to settle down. His mother and two married sisters were hounding him too. Although there was no shortage of candidates, marriage was a lifelong commitment, and he had to choose wisely. He sought God for guidance to find the right woman. As a committed Christian, there were assets he was looking for hidden to the naked eye—her faith, love, and trust in the Lord Jesus. Plus, she had to know how to pray until she heard from God. In other words, he wanted a woman who was committed to a lifetime of walking with the Lord. He had seen too many of his buddies' marriages split because Christ wasn't the center. He didn't want to make the same mistake. In addition to his spiritual desires, Ashton was still a man in the flesh, and her looks had to be pleasing to his eyes.

"One day." He grunted, shaking off his wandering mind. Yet, he believed each day would bring him closer—face-to-face—to the woman who would be his wife. Lately, he couldn't stop thinking about a mate— blame it on the good weather that sparked pleasant thoughts or the intoxicating scent emulating from a box he was about to deliver. He had to stay focused because he was on a tight schedule. The overnight pre- loaders at the hub had stacked so many boxes in his vehicle, it would take him late into the evening to empty his truck.

Any other day of the week, he didn't mind getting home late. This evening was different. Not only was he looking forward to meeting other singles, but he hadn't stepped foot in a bowling alley in many years, so he was hyped about reconnecting with a sport he enjoyed as a teenager. He hoped against all odds he would finish early enough to go home, shower, and get to Strike-n-Spare.

Grabbing the box addressed to D. Hayes, he jumped out of the truck and did a trek across the driveway to the house. He rang the doorbell and placed the package on the porch. He never waited   for the owner to answer. It was a common courtesy to alert them, then he kept moving, especially today.

The door opened at the same time he stepped off the landing.

"Thank you," the sweetest voice called from behind him.

He was about to give the customary wave, but he glanced over his shoulder, and he froze, staring at the woman in the doorway. She had the "wow" factor. As she reached down to retrieve her package, Ashton raced back and beat her to it. The scent inside the box would suit her. "Sorry, ma'am."

The shade of blue she wore was now his new favorite color. She was striking. With one glance, he sensed her confidence and strong will. If she smiled, it would probably soften her features and he would be a goner. There was something sexy when a woman smiled, and even more alluring when she laughed. Involuntarily, he checked out her left hand—no ring.

Don't lose sight of what God has for you, he coaxed himself. *Does she fit His criteria for godly wife material?*

"No problem." Ashton nodded with a smirk.

He was attracted to women who wore dresses, since so many opted for jeans and pants these days. The flash of blue had already hypnotized him. To keep from surveying her legs, Ashton had focused on her face. She was very pretty. Her beautiful dark brown eyes were soulful. Every feature seemed to accent her face—from her short hair to the fullness of her mouth. He withheld his whistle.

Instead of jogging back to his truck, he showcased

his swagger—in case she was checking him out. Once he climbed behind the wheel, Ashton had to exhale a couple of times to regulate his heartbeat. In doing so, the remnants of the fragrance of her package teased his nostrils.

A woman's beauty hadn't knocked him off balance since he turned eighteen. He exhaled again. He had been on this route in North St. Louis County for two years and maybe he did drop off packages to her house before—he couldn't say. But after one look at her, he felt weak in the knees, and he was sitting down.

Not good. Didn't King David, his son Solomon, and strong man Samson fall to beautiful women? Shaking his head, he regrouped. "Okay, Satan, you're sending a decoy to the wrong man." Ashton started the motor and shifted his truck into gear. He didn't peek at the house again as he rounded the cul-de-sac and drove as far away from temptation as possible.

The solution to release him from the invisible headlock was to get to the singles ministry tonight and keep his eyes set on a Christian woman. Yet, as the day dragged on, he couldn't shake the image of D's face—he wished he knew her first name—from his memory.

Chapter 2

Bowling was a bust, despite the pep talk Minister Ray gave Dominique, Paige, and thirty others who boarded the church vans for their outing.

Pray for your mate as if he were standing before your eyes, their leader had said, citing Hebrew 11:1: *Now faith is the substance of things hoped for, the evidence of things not seen.*

No matter how often Dominique had blinked, neither she nor Paige had captured a man's attention longer than a "you're up next" summons.

For her, the night had yielded nothing more than an achy wrist from lifting what had to be a twenty-plus pound bowling ball. She didn't care if the so-called experts argued the balls couldn't weigh more than sixteen pounds. Her wrist said otherwise.

Now, a week later, she and Paige were still discussing their bowling-for-a- boyfriend fiasco at a sidewalk cafe in the Loop. Since her friend was between jobs, Dominique picked up the bill for lunch. While waiting for their orders, they people watched, chatting. The hot spot was a crossroads for city and suburban dwellers.

The sunshine, the breeze, the vibrant colors of flower gardens seemed to liberate her mind as she shed the hat, coat, boots and gloves that constrained her. As the seasons changed, so had Dominique's attitude concerning her impatience for a husband.

God had repeatedly whispered James 1:4 in her soul: *But let patience have her perfect work, that ye may be perfect and entire, wanting nothing.* So as spring yielded promises of good weather, she refused to go back into mental hibernation.

"I thought we were supposed to pray for our spouses after we got married. To pray for a faceless man now still seems eerie." Paige shivered. "Makes you wonder if he's a drug dealer, in prison, or homeless."

"It's definitely suspenseful," Dominique said. "Makes a woman wonder who God has chosen for her. It's almost like an arranged marriage at birth."

Paige snickered as their chicken fingers and fries arrived. "And our parents have been trying to get us married off for years."

They paused to give thanks for their meal, then Dominique spoke. "Yeah, the only problem is their taste in men. Mom wants a hunk, so she will have beautiful grandchildren, while Daddy wants a son-in-law who can pass a tool competency test."

"That's because you're an only child," Paige said. "I have two older brothers to add to the security detail. If I never get married, it would be fine with them."

"We need a distraction," Dominique said. "Remember our trip last year to Puerto Rico?" They both loved to travel and weren't intimidated about just the two of them going.

"Girl, yes, and I had no problem relocating with any of those brothers-in-Christ." She practically groaned as she dipped her chicken into her barbecue sauce. "We haven't skipped a beat since we started traveling three years ago and took Europe by storm…" Paige looked away, but not before Dominique witnessed the sadness flash across her face. "This year, I'm unemployed and basically homeless," her friend griped.

She rested her cup on the table and eyed her. "You might not have a job, but you're not homeless. I offered you my spare bedroom—rent free—for months, but you opted to move back in with your parents."

Paige shrugged. "You're my best friend—like a sister. I wasn't about to sabotage our relationship by being a roommate. You're neat, I'm semi-disorganized."

Dominique laughed. "You're junky."

"Untidy," her friend countered. "Anyway, the only trip I'm looking forward to is my family reunion in Phoenix."

"That's next summer."

"Honestly, all I want is to be gainfully employed—"

"I could use an administrative assistant." Dominique would create a spot for her friend, if only Paige would say the word.

"You know I wouldn't work for you either." Page shook her head. "When it comes to business, you'd fire me in a minute for not doing something your way."

Twisting her lips, Dominique smirked. "You know it, but for you, there would be a grace period— one day tops." Despite her teasing, she would do everything she could to keep Paige employed. Wiping her mouth, she noted the time, then asked the waiter for the check. "I have a late meeting across town, so I'd better get going."

They stood and exchanged hugs. "Are you going to be back in time for the singles meeting tonight?"

"I wouldn't miss sitting next to my imaginary husband."

Ashton couldn't shake his melancholy mood. It wasn't as if he was walking around with a bad attitude or anything, but lately nothing seemed to be going his way. First, he missed the bowling fellowship because of working late. He was beyond disappointed on so many levels, the first being he needed a distraction from the pretty face that had haunted his every idle minute.

Now his mind was stabbing him in the back because of D. Hayes. Weeks had passed and there had been no further deliveries for her or anyone on the street. Frustration was building, because he wanted to get another glimpse of the woman that he didn't want to think about.

Something about her still had a strong magnetic pull on his senses. He wondered how the perfume smelled on her skin. Was it bold, faint, or would the fragrance dissipate within hours?

After parking his car on the company lot, Ashton stole a deep breath and exhaled before opening the door. "I must be losing my mind," he mumbled before getting out. He couldn't shake this woman for anything. Of course, he didn't mention this to his family when he sat next to them at church on Sunday, especially his two sisters whose mission was for him to be happily married by now. "Whew."

Back up against the wall, Ashton did what any other practicing Christian man would do, he prayed for deliverance of this mental torment as he strolled inside the hub to get his truck and list.

"Hey, Ash," Burt Dunlap, the shift supervisor, called out to him as his best friend joined his stride to the counter.

"Ready for the open road?" was Marc Gillis' usual morning greeting without fail.

"You know it," Ashton had to force himself to reply with his standard saying. Maybe he was coming down with something? Working his head from side to side, he refocused on the task at hand. He liked his job at Package Express, the nation's second largest logistic company.

To some, making deliveries might seemed mundane, but he enjoyed not being tied behind a desk for eight hours—in his case, sometimes ten, depending on the workload. Plus, lifting boxes and sometimes outrunning loose dogs kept Ashton in shape.

Climbing in his truck, he booted up his tablet to peruse his scheduled deliveries. He almost hyperventilated when two addresses on Rosedale Circle appeared on his list, but neither were for Hayes. Ashton smiled anyway.

For some unexplained reason, his day just improved. He delivered each package with diligence knowing he was one address away from his desired destination. By mid-afternoon when he turned into D. Hayes' subdivision, Ashton's palms were sweaty. As he barreled down the street, he slowed, blinking. Not only was he not expecting to see her at home, but wobbling on crutches to her mailbox either. Ashton drove past his scheduled drop-offs and pulled in front of her, then shifted into park.

"Hey," he yelled, jumping out of his truck. "Looks like you need some help."

"I do." She looked relieved.

He took her mail and assisted her back to her porch. Gone was her professional attire. Instead, she was casually dressed in a T-shirt and capris. He peeped at the thick bandage secured around her ankle. He didn't stop there as he scanned the shape of both legs—nice. The unmistakable faint scent suited her.

"Looks like you had a fall," he joked as they

neared her front door.

"Yeah." She huffed. "Remind me never to try out for a softball team again."

They chuckled. "Deal. If at any time in the future, I see you have deliveries from Major League sports, I'll keep driving."

She graced him with a smile that made his jaw and heart drop at the same time. *Wow*. He saved himself the embarrassment of drooling as he opened the storm door and waited for her to step up inside her foyer. After making sure she was steady on her feet, Ashton handed over the mail.

"Thanks again," she said, a little out of breath. So was he. "Oh, by the way, I have a box of paper that should come tomorrow."

"Noted." He grinned and backed away. When she closed the door, he jogged to his truck. *Come on tomorrow*. Not since his first day on the job thirteen years ago had Ashton looked forward to work. What was it about D. Hayes that had him discombobulated? She had many physical assets, but her smile did him in. He was a goner for sure.

He realized he'd better tread lightly, because many great men had fell when it came to beautiful women. "Lord, help me."

Chapter 3

Dominique Hayes had a package, Ashton learned the next morning when he scanned his delivery list on his truck. He repeated her name above a whisper. Did he know any Dominques? If any had crossed his path, they had faded from his memory.

Scanning Miss Hayes' name was stirring up conflict in his mind. What was her draw that had him paying more attention to his grooming the previous night?

With meticulous precision, Ashton had shaved and trimmed his beard; clipped the gray strands from his eyebrows, and contemplated applying dental white strips—he did. Lastly, he rubbed the curls in his hair, which could only be tamed by a wave cap until he could get to a barber. He said his prayers for wisdom on his actions, then fell asleep. Yeah, it was going to be a great day.

His sisters, Felicia, the oldest, and Bailee, the youngest, said women liked men in uniforms—basically their friends they tried to set up with him. But Ashton was on to their shenanigans. His desire was a godly woman or nothing, so which column would he place Dominique?

"Man, you're grinning awfully big this early." His coworker snuck up behind him, invading his thoughts.

Startled, Ashton shifted in his seat and recovered. "What's up, Marc?" Lifting his device, he acted as if nothing was out of the norm. "Going over my load."

Marc eyed him with feigned suspicion. "Maybe we should switch routes. I could use a short day." He chuckled.

That was a joke. As union drivers, overtime kept their yearly pay tipping over one hundred thousand dollars. Besides the basic living expenses, he lived within his means and banked extra or came to the aid of his widowed mother.

A light load meant a driver would have to assist fellow drivers to get in his eight hours. But money wasn't everything all the time. He'd much rather have a social life that involved church activities, not just Sunday service.

"Nah, I got this. I'm looking forward to the great weather on the open road." They chatted a few minutes and parted ways.

He thought about his job again. The company was stable with pension, 401(k), savings, and more.   Plus, his late father had provided for his family of five on a union salary. However, overtime had caused him to miss the bowling events and countless other church functions.

What he wanted most was to have a good marriage like his parents, and by all outward appearances, his sisters too. Getting a wife was easy. Finding the right one would take a lot of prayer.

Throughout the day, he spied the white box from Staples designated for Rosedale Circle. The countdown began with each drop-off until he was blocks away, unloading his truck at Nancy's Flower Pot.

Ashton had weekly deliveries there. The owner was an elderly lady with short white hair. She always had a ready smile outlined by pink lipstick. "How's my favorite driver today?" Her gray eyes sparkled with her shameless flirting. He was hoping his shorts, which he began to wear this time of year, wouldn't catch her attention.

"I always was a leg woman. I can tell you run or bike," she had said with no regard for embarrassing him. For that reason, Ashton focused on getting in and out in record time.

"Real good, Miss Nancy." He handed over his device for her to sign. Most of her deliveries required signatures. As he waited, sweet fragrances teased his senses until the urge to buy overpowered him with a risky idea. "I'd like to purchase those flowers, please." He nodded to the selection inside the cooler behind her.

She twirled around and pointed to about three of

them before she grabbed the right one on the second shelf. "The 'Let's Be Friends' bouquet." She nodded. "'Bout time. This is on me, young man."

"Oh no." Ashton wasn't having it. "Anything worth having is worth paying for." He thought about King David and Araunah in 2 Samuel 24:24: *I will surely buy it of thee at a price: neither will I offer burnt offerings unto the LORD my God of that which doth cost me nothing. So David bought the threshing floor and the oxen for fifty shekels of silver.* "Not this time. I can't take a lady flowers that I didn't personally invest in."

A whimsical expression crossed Miss Nancy's face before she exhaled. "Well said." She got to work after he glanced at his watch.

"Can't keep her waiting."

As she expertly wrapped the arrangement in white paper, she causally quizzed him about Dominique, but Ashton only had one answer. "I don't know much about her except she's pretty."

"Good start." She rang up his purchase, took his payment, and wished him good luck as he left.

Ashton didn't operate on luck. His actions were led by God's will. At least, he hoped so in this case. He never approached a woman unless he knew her status upfront, which he didn't. Suddenly, out of nowhere, doubt smacked him. There was basic information he needed to know before pulling this stunt. First, was she a practicing Christian baptized in water and filled with the Holy Ghost fire? Was Dominique married, but not wearing her ring the day he saw her? He was also playing a dangerous game   if

19

she was living with a man.

"What was I thinking?" Hesitation replaced anticipation when he parked at the curb in front of her house. What sounded like a good idea less than thirty minutes earlier now seemed flawed. He was stepping out of the vehicle, contemplating whether he should or shouldn't, when he saw her teetering in the doorway.

He raced to the door when it seemed she was about to topple over. "Hey, are you okay?"

She nodded. "I was hoping you brought my paper." She glanced toward the truck.

"I did." He exhaled and stared at her to make sure his memory was right. Yes, she was beautiful. Tilting her head, she gave him an odd expression. "Ah, when I thought you were about to fall, I came to your aid."

Her lips curled. "Oh, thank you."

The smile did him in. *God, help me.* "I'll get that now. Besides your box of paper, I have a floral delivery for you too." He tried to sound casual while watching her expression under the hood of his lashes.

She blinked a couple of times, then puckered her lips into an "o" and stuttered, "Wow. Flowers? Who would send me flowers?"

Ashton held his breath. He wanted to know that too. He shrugged and played it off. "I guess your husband, the boyfriend, or a secret admirer?" Boy, he was glad he'd left the card unsigned. If she answered yes to any one of them, her neighbor may be getting the flowers or his mother. But how was he going to get out of the jam?

"No husband or boyfriend. And if he's an admirer, he shouldn't keep it a secret."

20

He exhaled. *Good answer.* He stepped off the porch and headed to his truck. He returned with both packages, but Dominique only eyed one.

"Do you mind bringing the box inside and setting it on the desk?" She cautiously stepped back for him to enter while she lifted the flowers out of his arms with no regard for her balance.

Ashton stood ready to shield her from a fall as he performed a quick scan of her home. Her office was the first room off the foyer. His chivalry wasn't necessary as she seemed quite adapt on the aluminum sticks.

He noted the decor of light colors and large windows, allowing plenty of sunlight and a great view of her neighborhood. The place was so neat, it didn't look lived in. She definitely didn't have children.

On a glass desk, her papers and things were organized. "There you go." He set the box on a file cabinet the same height as her desk.

She ignored him as she ripped apart the paper around the bouquet and buried her nose in it. From the smile and glow on her face, Ashton guessed he had done well. She reached for the card and read it, "Hoping for a speedy recovery." *Hmmm.* "There's no signature." She pouted.

"Have a good day." He made a quick exit, too tongue-tied to speak up. Minutes later, behind the wheel, Ashton chided himself for his sudden bashfulness. Back at the hub, Marc commented on his aloofness until Ashton confided about his missed opportunity. "I was standing right in front of her, man." He gritted his teeth in frustration. "I   should've told her I was the sender."

"Do you know how many fine chicks I have on my route? Zero." Marc emphasized with his fingers. "Just old folks working in the yard or sitting on their porches. I would have asked for her number."

"Forget a number. If she was as fine as you say, I would have tested the waters for an afternoon delight." Tom Kelly had a knack for eavesdropping, then offering an unsolicited opinion. Their coworker was the father of two and had no problem sleeping with women who weren't his wife.

He and Marc gave the other driver an annoyed glare. "You give brothers a bad rap. Be faithful to the one you got, man." Ashton frowned. *Why make a vow and not mean it?* He had witnessed to Tom about Jesus' love, salvation, and soon return, but his fellow driver was draining. He had little regard for his life now or after.

Steering Marc to the parking lot to their vehicles, Ashton finished his conversation. They were alike in so many ways, including liking their jobs and keeping their personal life private in a business setting. "I believe God will show me a woman who loves Him and who will love me." He was serious about his search for a wife—a committed Christian. And God must have piqued an interest in Dominique for a reason. "I don't know if that was the Lord leading me earlier, but I would like to find out before I make an idiot out of myself again."

Marc laughed. "Something tells you you'll get your second chance as long as there is Amazon and other websites that use our company."

Chapter 4

"You got what?" Paige asked Dominique over the phone.

"Flowers," Dominique whispered as if she weren't alone in her own house. "I'll snap a picture and send it."

"Wow, I don't know if I should be jealous or encouraged that I could be next." Her friend had the same awe in her voice as Dominique had when she first saw the flowers. "I guess praying for your husband called him out from hiding,"

Dominique *tsk*ed. "Girl, I can buy myself flowers. It's the husbands we can't seem to get free. The delivery guy said they were from a secret admirer." She gnawed on her lips, wracking her brain on who the suitor might be until panic struck. "Wait a minute.

23

How does this person know where I live? Am I under surveillance?" Her heart began to pound with fear.

"Now who's the drama queen?" Paige paused. "Let's do the process of elimination. Maybe it was the hunk who carried you to the bench when you injured your ankle. We did provide our contact information in the singles group. Maybe you listed your address."

Dominique twisted her lips. "Not good. Plus, Mr. Fine seemed more interested in getting me off the field to continue the game than my condition. Who's next on the list?"

"That's all I've got so far."

"So much for brainstorming," she mumbled, frowning until she glanced at the arrangement again, then smiled. The flowers were vibrant and full.

"You have to admit it's romantic." Paige sighed.

"Or scary," Dominique countered, looking over her shoulder, expecting to see someone with binoculars peering in her window. Since she didn't own and was fearful of guns, she needed a guard dog ASAP. Maybe she could get one of them delivered. "If I get something else from this secret stalker, I'm calling 9-1-1."

Am I not your fortress? Put your trust in Me, and I'll hide you in the shadow of My wings, God whispered from Psalm 91.

The Lord's words relaxed her. A shadow was a reflection of something real, yet the Lord's shadow held strength, so there was nothing for her to fear. When she moved out the house, her mother made her memorize hundreds of Scriptures about overcoming fear. Most she had forgotten, but many lingered in her heart, and living alone had never bothered her before.

Her friend chuckled. "It's only scary if the flowers are dead or black. I can't wait to see them in person. After weeks of no bites, what are the odds of me landing two job interviews on the same day? I'll drop by after my two interviews tomorrow!" she practically screamed. "No calls, then all of a sudden two on one day. I'll even bring you something to eat for lunch."

Dominique smiled. "Ooh, company! Can't wait." And she couldn't, especially to see her best friend. Her mother calls and visits since her injury didn't count. She and Paige lived in opposite sides of St. Louis. The short half hour drive didn't stop them from getting together at least once a week outside of church activities.

Paige worked overtime to find another position in her field of interior design. Dominique rocked in her office chair and admired her open floor plan, which Paige had helped design. Her condo was a refuge after a hectic day at work. The two of them had an adventure decorating it. The outcome garnered praises and business. Her friend was good at what she did. Paige needed to be at a company that appreciated her vision.

Dominique didn't possess a creative gene. But she did excel in her job as senior accounts manager with Global Payroll Systems. Her injury was a setback on meetings with prospective clients that her executives were counting on her to sit in with them to help win the bids. She was driven, professional, and now bored, not liking what she considered to be on "house arrest" confinement all because she was running at top speed to get to home plate.

Dominique glanced at the flowers again before tackling another round of emails. Maybe Paige was right. The flowers could be from the captain of their softball team. Dominique did feel a special connection with Brother Branch. After all, he assigned her to first base, which she thought was prime real estate—until she overheard someone say it was given to the slowest and least experienced player.

Really? she thought. Dominique was determined to show her teammates she had skills and a competitive spirit, so she guarded her post like a pit bull.

"You're a pro, Sister Shortstuff," Brother Branch *had said with a wink after she had caught the softball and tagged two players out as first base.*

Anybody else calling her petite height short would have gotten corrected, but considering he was six foot five, all muscle, and towered over her, she took shortstuff as his endearment.

And to think she had complained when she got into Paige's car early last Saturday morning.

"Something is definitely wrong with this picture." Dominique adjusted the temperature and blasted the heat as she shivered.

Paige chuckled and her hazel eyes twinkled. "Well, good morning to you too." Once Dominique clicked her seatbelt, her friend drove off. "What do you mean?"

Leaning on the headrest, Dominique shook her head. "The Bible says, he who finds a wife, finds a good thing and obtains favor from God."

"O-okay, so what's with the Proverbs 18:22?"
Paige shrugged. *"Every single Christian woman can
quote that Scripture."*

"I'm thinking—"

"Scary." Paige giggled.

*"No, seriously. If our future husbands are looking
for us, shouldn't Minster Ray pick activities like a
ballet, an art museum, or cooking class? My wrist still
hurts from lifting that bowling ball."* She dangled her
hand in the air to illustrate. *"Now, we're heading to
the park to form a softball team with two other
churches singles ministries."*

*It wasn't that she didn't like sports. She preferred
to watch them from the stands or her sofa. Her daily
exercise was a long walk or utilizing her home gym.*

*"We've done all those things together—you and
me—"* Paige pointed to herself then Dominique, *"and
single brothers don't hang out there."* Paige sighed,
exiting on to I-270 East toward Spanish Lake. *"I guess
if the brothers won't come to us, we'll have to meet
them on their own turf."* She grinned.

"No, the pun didn't work." Dominique snickered
and glanced out the window. *"You know, even if we
don't meet a special someone, we have to give
Salvation Temple, Jesus Only Church, Redemption
Fellowship, and even Corinthian Church singles
ministries kudos for organizing these events for us."*

"You'll get a loud Amen from me on that."

Less than a half hour later they arrived at Fort
Belle Fontaine Park. Dominique's heart pounded with
wonder. Would her husband-to-be be waiting for   her

at home plate?

After greeting familiar and new faces with "Praise the Lord," she and Paige climbed into the stands to wait team assignment and other instructions. Dominique thought she and Paige were stunning in their red and blue capris, long-sleeved T-shirts, and coordinated wind jackets, so why weren't they getting picked in the first round?

"Girl, if they don't choose us soon, I'm quitting." Paige gave her a side-eye.

"Sister Dominique Hayes from Salvation Temple, George Cain, and Kevin Williams from Jesus Only Church," Brother Branch, singles leader at Redemption Fellowship, read from a list on the clipboard. "And Sister Paige Blake from Salvation."

Brother Branch had named his team of fifteen Warriors for the Lord. The other team was called Army of the Lord. The real perk was the brothers outnumbered the sisters on her team.

Unlike bowling, Dominique was really enjoying herself, especially since she was outperforming other sisters athletically throughout five innings. She let down her guard and just had fun. She realized maybe she was having too much of a good time when her team was up at bat. When it was her turn to hit, she judged a ball she'd hammered was destined for a homerun score. Despite Brother Branch's call for her to stay at third base, Dominique felt she could make it.

That was before she realized the six-foot sister from Jesus Only Church was waiting for her at home plate with her game face on. It was too late to back track, so she braced for impact. The collision   wasn't pretty. When Dominique opened her eyes, her cute clothes were soiled, and pain was piercing her ankle. She flinched thinking about it, then the flowers caught her attention and she blushed.

"It's all right. I gotcha, Sister Shortstuff," *Brother Branch lifted her in his arms like a baby and gently carried her to the bench. "Can we get some ice and a health professional to make sure she's all right?" he yelled impatiently.*

Without waiting, he'd jogged to the field without a backward glance.

The game had resumed and he never looked her way again, so maybe it was guilt that caused him to seek her out with flowers.

The next day, Dominique blinked as she peeked out the window, balancing her weight on the crutches. The familiar truck was parked outside.

Not only hadn't she ordered anything, but from being homebound, Dominique knew the truck didn't come through her neighborhood this early. Could it be another gift from Brother Branch? It was the same man.

It hadn't gone unnoticed at first glance. He was built and nice-looking—no, handsome. He worked the uniform. This time when she opened the door, her eyes strayed to his ring finger. But its absent ring didn't mean anything anymore. *You promised God only a practicing Christian will be your focus,* her conscience took her to task. *Be on guard.*

The man stood at attention. Instead of a bulky box, he held a clear container with a lunch from the local grocer, Dierbergs. She eyed the package, then him. She pointed. "I know there are strict guidelines about shipping food, so what's going on? Who is paying for this service?" She rambled off questions until he chuckled. Nice white teeth against his dark skin. Wow!

"I'm Ashton Taylor. Since you're mending, I thought you might enjoy lunch." He seemed to exhale at the same time she did. Was it a good thing to know her stalker? *Okay, stop it.* Her imagination did an abrupt halt when she realized she was ogling him. Ashton had to lift weights.

She was so flattered, flustered, and speechless, she had to recover before introducing herself. "Ah, I'm Dominique Hayes, but you probably already know that, huh?" His eyes seemed to dance as she blushed and her heart fluttered. "Thank you. So the flowers were from you?"

"Yes." His expression was intense as if he was trying to read her emotions. "I have to get back to my deliveries, but if you need anything, let me know. I will gladly pick it up while I'm on this route." He reached in his shirt pocket, pulled out a receipt from somewhere and a pen, then scribbled his number on it. "Please call me."

Not if you're not God sent. She debated accepting his gift, but did. She was even more hesitant about the paper with his number, unless she needed a package pickup. Once she closed the door, Dominique tried to process what had just happened.

She honestly didn't know what to make of his gesture. She hobbled back to her desk. Easing into her chair, she examined the box, scrutinizing the package for signs of tampering. Turkey, ham, roast beef, and Swiss cheese on rye. She wasn't a fan of sub sandwiches, but she was hungry. The gourmet cupcake inside won her over. Satisfied the seal hadn't been broken, she elevated her foot again and called Paige. "You don't need to bring me lunch—my secret admirer did."

"Revealed!" she screamed. "How does Mr. Jimmy John look?" she teased, referring the sandwich restaurant known for its speedy delivery commercials.

"Like my delivery driver."

"No way! After this second interview, I am so on my way. I'll get me something off the value menu, then join you. I want to hear all about it." They disconnected.

Dominique sighed. If nothing else, Ashton had saved Paige from spending money she didn't have. Her friend didn't want pity and would give, even if she had little.

An hour later, Paige used her key and let herself in. "Hey, Dom. It's me."

"In the kitchen," Dominique yelled from her perch at the table.

After exchanging hugs, Paige rested her purse on the counter along with her hamburgers, then circled the vase of flowers. Next, she spied Dominique's lunch.

"Maybe I should spend the night to see if he'll bring two candlesticks tomorrow for a romantic dinner."

"Funny. He gave me his number, if I need something." Dominique shook her head. "I'm not calling that man."

Paige didn't reply as she washed her hands, then sat at the table. Bowing her head to say grace, Dominique followed, and they asked Jesus to bless their food.

After a couple of bites, Paige eyed her. "So, you're not calling him, huh? What does he look like?"

"Handsome, wavy hair, a thin beard that I hadn't noticed the first time…white teeth…tall…muscular… Dominique listed each asset. "In a suit and tie, he probably would be jaw-dropping fine." She sighed, creating that image in her head.

"Not a beard." Paige closed her eyes and smiled. Her friend was attracted to men with facial hair—from a five o'clock shadow to a goatee and anything in between. To her, a clean-shaved man looked boyish. She held out her hand. "Pass over his number. I'll call him."

From Paige's poker face, Dominique didn't know if she could trust her friend not to flirt with the guy, but calling Ashton then forcing Dominique to talk to him. She shook her head.

After finishing up her third Jack in the Box taco, Paige wiped her mouth and patted the table as if she was ready to get down to business. "So, what's your take? Could this Ashton be a decoy from the devil or a blessing from God? Minister Ray said to pray for our spouse as if he was in front of us." She *tee-hee*d. "It couldn't get any better than standing on your porch."

"Funny." Dominique licked the icing from the cupcake off her top lip. "I think you're reading way too much into this. It was a simple gesture." She frowned. "Right?"

Paige smirked and shrugged. "I wonder who God is sending my way. I mean doesn't the Scriptures say stand still and see I'm God or something? We're running around trying to find husbands and one knocks at your door."

"Excuse me. You're getting carried away. How did a deliveryman suddenly become husband material?"

"Flowers and food," Paige pointed out. "That automatically puts him in the running, but maybe my imagination is running wild. Regardless, we're supposed to lead people to Christ. That isn't an option. Invite Ashton to a singles event with no heartstrings attached."

Dominique nodded. "I don't know if I can invite another man to church without hopeful expectation, but I'll think about it."

Chapter 5

"I thought she would call by now," Ashton confided to his coworker who he knew he could trust. But after two days of waiting, she hadn't.

"Well, you tried, buddy." Marc slapped him on the back. "Buy a woman flowers and lunch, then nothing."

"Yeah," Ashton had agreed and headed home. Surprisingly, it was early enough to make it to his Friday singles night out service where he could refresh his soul.

Corinthian Church was small compared to some of the mega churches in the area with about two thousand active members. There were plenty of sisters for him to be married by now and have children. But he hadn't met "the one" yet.

His younger sister, Bailee, had taken a chance, marrying a man who hadn't stepped foot into a church since grade school, and it worked out when he surrendered to Christ, and they appeared happy with a daughter. Ashton wasn't willing to take that chance with his love life. His father and grandfather had been a minister and deacon, respectively. His future wife had to be a committed Christian, so they could grow together.

He thought as he cleared the entrance to the church that his heart and head would stop pining over Dominique. He didn't know the woman past her sweet smile and where she lived. He exhaled, and his heart settled as he stepped into the sanctuary. "Home," he whispered as he strolled to his familiar spot near a couple of other single brothers.

They shook hands before he sat on a pew and bowed his head in prayer to give thanks to God for being inside the sanctuary another day. Soon, the praise team kicked off the service with their rendition of "My Soul Has Been Anchored in the Lord," followed by a few a congregational songs.

The praise was still high when the singles leader, Minister Jackson Summers, took the microphone. "Seasons change and so do circumstances in our lives. One thing should remain constant, regardless of what we go through. If we walk in the Spirit, then we won't fulfill the lust of the flesh.' Galatians 5:16 is not only one of the golden texts of the Bible for all practicing Christians, but especially for singles where the temptation is great. The struggle is real, our emotions and affections are real, but let me encourage you to hold on. Remember, without holy living, no man shall see the Lord."

Minister Summers exhorted the audience with examples of victorious living before concluding with a portion of 1 Samuel 16:7: *"Man looks on the outward appearance, God judges the hearts.* Pray that your future wife or husband has a pure heart and in turn, give her or him a pure heart."

The altar call for salvation was extended, the offering was collected, and the benediction was given. As customary, they grouped off to continue their fellowship over food at a restaurant. If Ashton hadn't heard the encouraging message, he would have declined, but he needed to be among like-minded singles.

About twelve of them decided on CJ Muggs. Once there, the brothers were outnumbered by the sisters two to one. Ashton could feel the subtle flirts, but he would do as Minister Summers suggested and keep a pure heart. Too bad Miss Dominique Hayes wasn't among them, because he sure wanted to know if she was worth the mental torture she unwittingly was putting him through.

One thing was for sure. If she had another package, he wouldn't linger at her front door.

"Girl," Paige fumed after service on Sunday, "if you don't call him, I'll go online and order everything

I've ever wanted for Christmas, use your credit card, and have it delivered to your house."

Dominique tried to play off Paige's tantrum. After all, they were still in the church's parking lot after Sunday's worship service. The message was uplifting and here her friend was trying to flip the script on her. "Why can't we just leave it as he meant well, because I was on the mend, which is what he said. That was four days ago. I doubt he works on Sundays." She exhaled.

When Dominique began to huff while maneuvering her crutches to Paige's car, her friend slowed her steps. "If a cashier who had double bagged my groceries then gave me his number to call for home deliveries, you would be this persistent too, huh?"

"Maybe." She shrugged, then helped Dominique inside the car. "If a man brought me flowers and lunch, I would definitely pay attention."

Once Dominique was strapped in, she waited for her friend to get behind the wheel. Facing her, she explained, "You know how many guys have tried to hit on me and they don't have ten bucks in their sagging pants pockets? They see money, no ring, and hope I'm desperate for any man."

Paige gave her a tender smile. "This could be different. None of those losers who weren't wearing a suit and tie did something that sweet, and the ones in the suits and ties wanted you as their showpiece." Dominique said nothing, so her friend continued, "You know nothing happens by chance. God wanted you and that man's paths to cross." Paige grinned,

37

then started her engine and drove off the lot. "I'm inviting myself to your house for dinner, and I'm treating."

Laughing, she squinted her eyes. "How does my house and treating sound like a perk to me?"

"Because I'm cooking while you call Ashton." When Dominique geared up to protest, Paige cut her off.

"Ooh. I can't wait until the tables turn and you're in my seat, so I can badger you. Bully."

Over dinner of mashed potatoes, asparagus, and leftover meatloaf, they discussed Paige's upcoming call-back interviews. "I'm praying God will open up the door soon as it appears He has for you." She grinned, but Dominique wasn't taking the bait as she continued to change subjects.

Once they cleaned the kitchen, they lounged in her living room, and Dominique counted the seconds before Ashton's name came up again

"Enough stalling. Call him." Paige stood, reached for the phone and planted it in Dominique's hand.

After locating the receipt with his number, Dominique swallowed back her anxiety as her heart pounded. All while Paige anchored her elbows on her knees and leaned forward, watching like an expectant puppy for his chow.

Surprisingly, Ashton answered on the second ring. Although she had seen him, it was his phone voice that caused her to suck in her breath. *Wow. Stay focused,* she coaxed herself as Paige tilted her head and lifted a brow with a smirk. "Hello…" She cleared her throat. "This is—"

"Miss Dominique Hayes," he finished with a softness in his voice that she could imagine matched a warm expression.

Removing the phone from her ear, she squinted at it before placing it back. "Caller I.D."

"No. Yours showed unknown." He paused. "To be honest, I was hoping you would call days ago. How are you?"

If he was scolding her, she couldn't tell. "Getting stronger every day. I didn't know drivers delivered flowers and lunch." She chuckled and so did he.

"We deliver everything a customer is willing to ship. This time I became the sender and hand delivered my package."

"So how often do you do this?"

He was quiet, and she didn't think he was going to answer. Paige stood, gave her a thumbs-up and mouthed, "My job here is done. Call me."

Dominique's wave was more of a shooing Paige out the door as she snuggled deep into her chaise.

"Never," Ashton said, sounding apologetic. "When I saw you, I thought you were pretty. I still do. I prayed and took a chance that you weren't married or involved and that my actions wouldn't scare you so bad that you reported me."

His flattery made her blush. A praying man. Plus, there was something rather sweet about a man willing to risk his livelihood for a chance. She wouldn't be a native St. Louisan without asking, "What high school did you attend?" Supposedly, a person's worth was determined by where they grew up and whether they were educated at city schools or prestigious suburban institutions.

"Webster Groves. My family has deep roots in that area that began after slavery." He paused. "Maybe, one day I can tell you stories passed down how my great-great-grandmother was the first black teacher in a segregated school system."

Family pride. She liked that. "Maybe, so what church do you attend?"

"Corinthian Church."

Dominique almost dropped the phone in disbelief—a sister church who declared the same mission statement that salvation was in no other name but Jesus. She was surprised they had never met at a district event, revival, or the recent outing.

"And you?" he asked.

"Salvation Temple." She exhaled and heard him do the same. "Are you part of the singles ministry? We recently fellowshipped with them at Strike-n-Spare. Were you there?"

"Unfortunately, no. I work a lot of overtime, and sometimes I get off too late to make it to outings." He chuckled. "I can't believe we would have met that night."

Recalling the night and remembering how packed the bowling alley had been, Dominique knew she blended with the crowd and didn't stand out. "I doubt you would have noticed me."

"Trust me, I wouldn't have been the only one. Wow." He chuckled. "I think I prefer the one-on-one interaction. How about dinner and a movie once you feel up to it? You choose where you would like to go."

She grinned. "All right. Fifty-four seventy-eight

Holman Drive."

"What saint of God doesn't know Salvation Temple is on Holman?" She could hear the humor in his voice. "The spiritual food alone is worth the dining experience."

Yes, her church's reputation was well known. Her pastor preached from the Bible. He didn't compromise or sugarcoat the Scriptures. If God said it, Pastor Nicks repeated it. "So, do you have a choice to work overtime, or is it mandatory?"

"It all depends on how you look at it. Boxes have to be picked up, others dropped off. I have to stay until the job is done."

"Hmm. I'm hearing expect canceled dates." She twisted her mouth, feeling disappointed.

"Nope. It means I may be late, but I would never cancel a date with you."

Dominique smiled, and her heart fluttered. "We'll see. How about this Friday?"

"It's a date."

Chapter 6

"Not good," Ashton chided himself as he traveled across the city to assist another driver who couldn't handle a large pickup. The request for backup wasn't out of the norm. The problem was he had a hot date. He worked the calculations in his head. It was two-thirty. It would take him thirty minutes to get to the college campus. Half an hour to load up and another forty minutes to get back to the hub. He didn't account for an accident on I-170 and then construction on Forest Park Parkway.

Since he had agreed to the church date, it was all he could think about. He had been the last customer at his barber before it closed the previous evening. Today, Miss Nancy at the flower shop insisted he purchase a journal from her rack of knick-knack items along with the single rose. The only reason he bought it was because it contained daily Scriptures.

There was something about Dominique that controlled his senses.

All day, he imagined joining her at church for the singles meeting. He couldn't wait to sit next to her and whiff her perfume as they shared a Bible—hers or his. It didn't matter.

Afterward, he would take her or she could trail him to Midnight Snacks in St. Charles, ten minutes or less from Lambert Airport, crossing on the Missouri River. He just wanted to be in her presence.

Ashton arrived on location and parked behind Gary's truck. Once he retrieved his dolly, he took the elevator to the second-floor lobby. "This is the last load I can fit in," Gary said. "Thanks for helping." Toting away what he could, the driver disappeared in the elevator.

He couldn't believe the chaos of stuff to be shipped. The college was sponsoring an alumni function in Florida the following week, so everything was slated for air freight. The time for takeoff was set and didn't budge. Ashton forgot what it was like to handle commercial pickups. Sometimes one truck wasn't big enough. He was amazed at the number and size of tubs and storage containers large enough for a body. He greeted the client with a smile while inwardly trying his best not to complain as he watched the time speed by.

At this point, he had two choices if there was any remote possibility that he could make it to Salvation Temple. The first one wasn't ideal, but to save face, he could freshen up at work, then head straight for church. Since he was sweaty and unkempt, that wouldn't make a good impression.

Even if he left the hub, rushed home, showered, and dressed appropriately, there was a seventy-five percent chance he would miss the service and Dominique. The last option was to pray the flowers he would send the next day would soften the blow.

At the moment, he didn't like his job.

"See, I told you he would come." Paige stuck out her tongue as they waited for Ashton to arrive at their church for the singles meeting event.

"Yes, you did." Dominique and Ashton had spoken for more than an hour that Sunday night until he reluctantly had to go so he could sleep.

Monday, he had called to check up on her and see if there was anything she wanted. His call had made her day, even though she declined. They were just beginning to talk, and she didn't want to encourage him to make frequent stops at her house uninvited.

On Wednesday, his continued concern made her giddy. "Will you let me know what the doctor says about your ankle?"

"I will as soon as my friend Paige brings me back home from the doctor." A few hours later, Dr. Parker cleared Dominique to put weight on her ankle again, but at a slow progression.

"I think it's sweet that he's concerned about you," Paige said as she parked in Dominique's driveway.

"It is. Thanks, sis, for the ride," she said, getting out of Paige's car. "But I better call Mom first."

"Of course," her friend said as they walked inside. Paige rummaged through her refrigerator for a snack while Dominique called her parents and texted Ashton, then she joined her friend in the kitchen.

An hour or so later, Dominique's doorbell rang.

"I'll get it," Paige practically sang on her way to the door. "Delivery." She strolled into the room with a big vase of colorful flowers.

Dominique's heart fluttered. "Was it Package Express?" she was about to jump up and head to the window when a pain shot through her ankle at the sudden movement. She gritted her teeth.

Paige set the vase on her table and came to her side. "You're only allowed one doctor's visit per day, and you've reached your limit." She frowned. "Would you be careful? And no, unless Ashton is a short white guy, driving a white truck, that wasn't him."

"Right." She reached for the envelope and read the card. *In all things, give thanks, so I give praise to Jesus for a good report. Ash.*

"Ash," she repeated and Paige whooped before she sobered.

"I hope my blessing comes soon."

Dominique patted her hand. "Me too." Maybe, Ashton has a friend—"

"Girl, I'm talking about a job."

"Oh." She squinted and watched her friend's expression.

"And then a man, of course." Paige cackled and Dominique talked too.

By the end of the work week, Dominique had mixed feelings about seeing Ashton again. She was nervous and excited. Their physical contact had been limited to business. She didn't know how she would respond to him face-to-face on a personal level.

The praise team was taking their places, so she hoped he would arrive soon. Taking a deep breath, Dominique exhaled as she scanned the audience. It was her night to show that a man was interested in her and he already was a practicing Christian—the bonus. If he looked halfway as handsome in a suit and tie or casual clothes as he did in a uniform, she would be the envy of every single sister there. But she had to wait for her turn to show off.

I resist the proud! God's voice thundered in her ear, drowning out the musical instruments. *Do not boast! Whether I give or take away, My name will be praised!*

Closing her eyes, she bowed her head. *Lord, I'm sorry for being puffed up. Please forgive me.*

You are forgiven.

Dominique's eyes teared as she exhaled. Getting to her feet, she stood next to Paige and lifted her hands and sung along with the praise team's rendition of Fred Hammond's "You Are My Daily Bread/Lord of the Harvest."

Twenty minutes later when Ashton still hadn't shown up, Paige nudged her. "Where is he?"

"Don't know. Probably at work." She squeezed her lips in disappointment. What a letdown.

"He'll be here," Paige said and patted her shoulder, probably reading her mind.

When they took their seats, Paige nudged her. "Hey, I haven't seen Sister Carr and that handsome guy in a few services. Rumors say she's pregnant."

"What?" Tears filled Dominique's eyes as her heart sank. "Pregnant," she repeated in a whisper. "Oh no."

Paige nodded with a sad expression. "Sin will happen when we take our eyes off the Lord, but God can keep us from falling."

Nodding, Dominique squeezed her friend's hand. Jude 1:24 was their constant companion when they faced trials. "Amen." Here she was ready to parade Ashton in front of the other single women and they had one who was hurting. "Sister Selma probably had hopes that the guy who she invited would be her husband. I noticed he stopped coming before she did."

"I know. I had to pray away the envy that was trying to build up inside me. I saw her get prayer after Bible class, and she seems so sad..."

Lord, please bless and comfort Sister Carr, and help us to be kind to her. In Jesus' name. Amen, Dominique prayed silently. Their sister-in-Christ wanted what every woman wanted, a good man for a good husband. Being a Christian woman narrowed their choices. "Let's pray he doesn't desert her, but surrenders his life to Christ," Dominique said.

When Minister Ray greeted them, Dominique glanced at her phone. No missed calls or texts from Ashton. At least she hadn't invested too much of her emotions in him.

"I know the focus of this ministry is to encourage spiritual purity while dating. As saints of God, we need to exercise spiritual purity in our hearts," Minister Ray cited Scriptures about God's love for about thirty minutes until he took questions from the audience. Afterward, he dismissed them to the fellowship hall where there were light refreshments.

"Hey, cheer up. I'm sure he had to work," Paige said as she lifted a cold bottled water out of a tub.

"I already don't like this uncertainty with him." Dominique didn't want to complain, especially after the sermon they'd heard, but it was ironic she'd met a practicing Christian man who seemed interested in her, but couldn't make it to church.

They didn't fellowship long. Paige probably sensed Dominique's mood and suggested they head home. "If you're up to company tomorrow, I can come over with popcorn and we can watch movies."

Dominique nodded. When her friend was employed, they filled their Saturdays with all-day shopping excursions, lunch, and a movie. Now, she accepted whatever activity Paige suggested.

As they gathered their purses and Bibles, they said their goodbyes. Two brothers were stationed at the doors to walk the sisters to their cars. When Dominique stepped outside, Ashton was strolling toward her. He made the black polo shirt and tan pants a fashion statement. His confident swagger was well noted. A bunch of flowers and a small bag was in one hand. She stumbled at the sight, causing him to quicken his steps to aid her. She recovered without his assistance. The wind stirred, and she caught a whiff of his cologne. She said nothing as they stared at each other.

Dominique noted the sadness in his brown eyes as he whispered, "I'm sorry."

When she debated whether to respond "it's okay" when it wasn't, Paige cleared her throat.

"You must be Ashton. I'm Dominique's best friend, Paige. Better late than never, huh?"

Dominique kept from rolling her eyes at her friend's attempt to lighten the moment.

Ashton didn't break eye contact with her as he spoke to Paige. "Nice to meet you."

Voices around them broke Dominique's trance. She could accept his apology, then what? It was a good thing they weren't meeting at a restaurant. She didn't want to think of the embarrassment and being left to pay the bill.

Forgive him, so that I will forgive you, God whispered. *Have you not read My Word in Matthew 6:14–15?*

Ashamed, Dominique lowered her head and silently repented.

Before she could respond, Ashton began hesitantly, "I could understand if you're mad at me. I had to work. It was too late for me to walk into service."

"So, you've been outside all this time?" Paige asked in awe, and Dominique frowned at her friend.

"Yes." Ashton never took his eyes off Dominique. "For you." He gave her the flowers and the bag. "It's a journal. Maybe you can write down everything you want to say about me, but won't say to my face."

She laughed for the first time. He was starting to know her so well. "It's okay. I guess I'm not used to that type of work environment, not knowing what time I get off." She began to walk toward Paige's car, and Ashton trailed.

"Sisters, is everything okay?" one of the doormen asked.

Turning around, Dominique nodded. "Yes. This is Brother Taylor from Corinthian Church."

The men exchanged greetings.

"Are you hungry?" he asked.

"Sure. They never serve enough food—" Paige said.

"We'll pass." She elbowed her friend. "Maybe, we'll talk tomorrow."

"Are you sure you're not going to change your number on me?" he joked.

"I won't."

Ashton held her in a trance, then nodded before he strolled away as she and Paige admired his swagger.

"I like him," Paige said. "Yep, he's perfect for you."

"He might be."

Chapter 7

Saturday morning, Dominique awoke after a restless night. All thanks to Ashton. Technically, he did stand her up for their first date. She lay there, staring at the ceiling. He had softened the blow with his sad puppy-dog expression. Plus, he had the nerve to come bearing gifts. She smiled. And the man had good taste in flowers. She'd give him that.

Wait a minute. Her smile turned into a frown. Dominique deserved better. If a man didn't have time to invest in a relationship… She didn't finish her thoughts as she scrambled out of bed in search of the journal Ashton had given her the previous night. She wanted to jot her ranting. None of the men who asked her out would have dared not to show up, then expect it was okay. She commanded respect and received it.

Unfortunately, those men weren't compatible with her spiritually.

What fellowship does lightness have with darkness? God whispered.

Second Corinthians 6:14 was the same Scripture that took her to task after the last guy—an attorney— she had walked away from. It wasn't that he wouldn't commit to her, it was the Lord and his philosophical views against Him.

Now that she had met a kindred spirit in the Lord, he wasn't dependable. Flopping on her chaise, which was poised in her bedroom by the bay window, she opened the journal, but held it to her chest. Gathering her thoughts, she connected her pen to the first sheet of paper. There was an inspirational quote at the top, but she didn't read it.

This isn't going to work, she began to scribble when the Holy Ghost intervened.

You've sought me for your heart's desire. Are you willing to throw it away?

"But is Ashton who I prayed for?"

Her mother had conditioned her with what to expect in a man since her first date as a teenager: "If you're not a priority when you're dating, that won't change if you marry him. When you see the red flag, cut your losses and get out because he won't change."

Dominique had carried that warning in her head with every man she'd dated, and it resurfaced the night before at church.

She had nothing invested in Ashton except a few phone calls, so it was still early enough to cut her losses. That was before Paige switched her allegiance the previous night. *"I still like him."*

"You don't know him," Dominique had argued.

"And you don't either. The simple fact that he is a saint of God is enough to give him a second chance to make a better impression."

Dominique didn't have a comeback. She had given the men who dressed in suits and ties, owned their own business or were upper management at their companies more chances. They seemed to be perfect for her and she had given them three or four shots at wooing her. They did a good job giving her all the attention she ever wanted, when she wanted it, but they always fell short when it came to the Lord. Now, things seemed to be flipped. Ashton walked with God, but he wasn't in control of his work schedule, so there was no way she could be a priority.

She and Paige had gone back and forth until Dominique agreed not to be too hasty.

The voices in her head distracted Dominique, but she was determined to be thorough in her assessment of the man.

What type of relationship do you want from me— friends or more? She let the questions roll. *Do you miss church a lot? What's the most important thing to you right now?*

When her stomach growled, she closed the journal and strolled to the kitchen to prepare oatmeal, then performed her morning regimen while it cooked on the stove.

She carried the journal in the kitchen and reopened it after she gave thanks for her food. *The flowers are nice gestures, but being a man of your word is better. Do you need a Scripture?* Dominique had to find one.

Putting it aside, she tidied the kitchen, then showered. She had just slipped on her clothes when Paige called.

"Have you spoken with Ashton?"

"Nope." She twisted her lips in defiance. "I'm not chasing him. He who finds a wife…"

At that moment, her phone beeped, and she recognized his number. "You talked him up." Paige didn't even say goodbye. She ended the call, and Ashton was there. "Hello."

"Are you still mad at me?" His deep voice was soft as if matching the sad look he had given her the previous night.

But this was how women got hurt, giving in too easily. "Should I be?"

"Yes, you should. Last night was important to me, too, but I pressed my way against the possibility that you may had already gone home. Still, I wanted to show you that no matter how late I am, I'll always be there."

Don't fall for it. "Those are sweet words, but…" She didn't finish.

"They're true, and if you want to chew me out, I'm man enough to take it. My only request is you do it in person over lunch."

She chuckled. The man was persistent. Dominique was torn. He intrigued her, but in one evening, he had annoyed her. Should she let his flattery win her over?

Yes, her heart answered.

"We can do soul food, salads, Asian, Italian—whatever your taste," he pressed her. "Then maybe we can walk off the calories with a stroll through the park. If you haven't written in your journal, bring it. Maybe we can write something in it together."

Ashton was breaking down her resistance as she peeped out the window and saw the few children in the neighborhood riding their bikes. With her windows cracked, smoke from someone's grill seeped into her house. "Do you like barbecue?"

He laughed. "What man doesn't?" "Have you ever eaten at Sugarfire Smoke House?"

"I haven't had a chance. I wouldn't mind experiencing my first visit with you. I know where it is. I can pick you up—" "I'd rather drive."

There was an awkward silence, then he agreed. "Before we go, can we pray?"

All the fight within Dominique dissipated. "Yes," she whispered and closed her eyes to let him take the lead.

"In the name of Jesus, thank You for waking us up this morning and forgiving us of our sins on Calvary. Now, as I try to woo Sister Dominique…"

She withheld her giggle.

"I ask that You guide me so she can see Your light in my life and the sincerity in my heart. In Jesus' name."

They whispered their Amens in unison. Prayer always had a calming effect on her, so she stopped fighting him. "See you at one p.m., and don't be late!" She had the last word and ended the call. "Okay, Lord. I like him." She screamed her excitement.

Chapter 8

Yes to God's beauty. Ashton stood when he saw Dominique glide across the parking lot. Her hips swayed in a denim dress that draped her curves and touched her knees. He appreciated the length, which showcased her legs. It was something he didn't see a lot of anymore as a man who admired legs, which was why in his opinion, pants weren't feminine. He didn't care how tight the skinny jeans were.

In the past, he thought he was attracted to women with the long hair—fake or God-given. Not anymore. Dominique's short style suited her and could seduce a man with one glance. Her short, sassy style seemed to fit her personality. Her true beauty was she walked with the Lord.

Folding his arms, he admired the air of confidence

with every step. She was probably unaware that she was the center of attention from some other guys not far from her. Ashton made his move when she noticed him. His long strides met her in seconds. Scanning her, he smiled as her polished toes peeped from her shoes.

"You are breathtaking." He reached out, and it was a good sign when she accepted his hand. It was soft and he felt a spark like sensation travel up his arm. He exhaled before speaking. "Praise the Lord. Thank you for coming."

In a surprising gesture, she bumped him with her shoulder. "You're going to pay up, brother. I'm double hungry from last night."

Squeezing her hand in a gentle grip, he barked out his amusement. "You can't break my bank. Trust me." Ashton had learned to stay away from women who were only interested in material gain from him, but Dominique seemed different, and he wanted to find out why.

He guided her inside the restaurant. After perusing the menu, he ordered a beef brisket sandwich, and she got pulled pork. Once they chose their sides, and received their orders, they decided to eat in the patio section.

Resting his tray, he pulled out her chair. He was close enough to inhale the scent of perfume, the same one that caused their introduction.

He took his seat. "What's the name of the fragrance you're wearing?"

She seemed surprised by his question. "It's an old one from Givenchy called Very Irresistible."

Just saying the words seemed to drug him. "Yes, you are."

Tilting her head, she smirked. "Are you always this charming?"

"According to my mother and two sisters, yes." He grinned. Linking his fingers, he anchored his elbows on the table and leaned forward. "Again, I'm sorry I missed our first date. It was on my mind all day. If you were as disappointed as me, then that's a good sign. So what was the message last night at the meeting?"

She frowned and twisted her mouth before chuckling. "I was so distracted, I can't even remember."

Wow. That tidbit made him feel worse. "Sorry to make you miss your blessing from God."

She nodded as her eyes twinkled. If only he could read her expression, then Ashton would know what she was thinking. "Did you bring the journal?"

"I did."

He reached across the table for her hands again. He bowed his head, then prayed the Lord would bless them and their food.

The hype this place got was well deserved he judged after the first bite. They ate in silence as Dominique seemed to study him. When it didn't appear she was going to share whatever she was thinking, he asked her about her job.

Her eyes sparkled and her shoulders relaxed. "I've worked for Global Payroll Solutions for six years. I've been blessed to win accounts others couldn't, and recognized with numerous awards."

Ashton was sure her stunning looks and the Lord's favor opened the door for her, but he didn't say that. He dared not suggest that to a woman as a compliment. According to his sisters, it was an insult to imply that a woman couldn't achieve accomplishments based on her own merit.

"I never thought I would like sales, but the competitiveness and unlimited earning potential with quarterly bonuses won me. So did meeting with clients and networking, because I'm a people person. Last year, I was promoted to senior account manager with four executives under my supervision. That was the Lord's grace that moved me in that direction." She paused. "Sorry, I'm rambling."

"I happen to enjoy your rambling. I like your expressive eyes, and love your energy." When she lowered her long lashes, he called her on that too. "And the way you blush." *Gorgeous.*

Balling up her napkin, Dominique tossed it at him.

He caught it with no effort. "Those sound like the same reasons why I like my job. The earning potential to the six figures, especially during peak times. I've met some interesting clients, but none as beautiful as you." His heart thundered against his chest when she lowered her lashes.

"When it comes to men and dating, I have high expectations."

"As a woman of God, I wouldn't expect anything less."

She looked away. Something was on her mind.

"I'm a patient listener," he said softly to coax her

to face him again. He touched her hand. "I want to earn your trust, Dominique."

He watched as she swallowed and then struggled. "I haven't always been in God's will when it comes to dating. I've kept my body pure—between the fear of God and my father—but not my mind. I've repented and don't plan to ever cross the line again."

He patted her hand. "The struggle is real for single folks. I've dated as well, but only sisters in Christ. Even there, we face temptations."

"I know," she said sadly. "One sister at my church just fell prey. It's sad."

"It is. I made up my mind a few years ago, only to date for one reason. To find a wife."

She blinked. The shock on her face was priceless. He withheld his amusement as he pulled her into a stare. Her breathing deepened. "All I ask of you is to give both of us a chance to get to know each other. Will you give me another chance?"

Dominique slowly pulled back. "I don't know what you're seeking in a wife, but for me, God has to be a priority for my husband, next me, and then building our relationship. That's non-negotiable." She lifted an eyebrow in a challenge.

He smirked. Didn't she know a man loved a challenge? Ashton leaned forward, closing some of the distance between them she had created. "Be careful what you ask for, Miss Hayes, because I'm the right man to deliver it. No pun intended."

Ashton thought he had fallen in love when he watched her lips open and the melodious sound of her laughter spill out. He joined her with a hearty laugh of his own.

Yeah, she was the one. Now, he had to prove to her that he was the only one for her.

Ashton Taylor was larger than life. Dominique did her best not to drool as he said what she wanted to hear, unknown to him.

"My family grew up in University City. How about a stroll through Lewis Park?"

"Sure." Dominique did her best not to sound too eager so soon, but she really enjoyed his company as he escorted her to her car.

"Nice ride." He nodded at her Toyota Mirai. "This suits you."

He was too on point about her, so now it was her turn. She scanned the parking lot. "Okay, let's see what looks like you."

He chuckled and folded his arms, never taking his eyes off her. "Give it your best shot."

She zoomed in on a monster pickup with a shine that blinded her. She pointed.

"Nope."

"*Hmph*ed." She cranked her neck. He didn't appear to be a convertible cruiser, so it had to be the Bravo SUV.

He laughed. "I drive a big truck at work. After hours, I like luxury, comfort, and something that doesn't remind me of work. When I clock out, I'm out of there. I don't take my work home."

Dominique couldn't say the same. Even on the weekends, she had to answer emails. She had a lot of freedom, but her hours weren't a structured nine to five.

"Give up?" When she nodded, he pointed to the Buick Lacrosse one aisle over. "Sure you don't want to ride with me? I have a superb driving record." He grinned, and his sex appeal climbed ten notches.

"I'm a single sister." She folded her arms and raised an eyebrow. "Don't you think I'm better safe than sorry? I'll drive and trail you." She smiled.

"Ahh, you'll definitely get along with my two sisters. You're fierce like them."

She almost said she looked forward to meeting them, but again Dominique held back. He opened her car door and waited until she was strapped in before closing it."

When he walked back to his car, she tapped Paige's number. "So far, so good. I like him."

"See. I knew you would."

"We're on our way to a park for a stroll. I'm scared to move too fast." He was not only handsome, but built like a linebacker, and he commanded his space like a bouncer. It was easy to feel safe around him.

"Keep praying, sister. You'll be okay."

"Got to go. He's waiting on me." She disconnected as she began following Ashton's black car eastbound on Olive Street, crossed over Midland, then passed University City's larger Hermann Park. She was surprised to see a park tucked away in a neighborhood off Delmar Boulevard. He parked, then waited for her.

"Did you bring the journal?"

She stepped out of the car and dragged her purse, which contained the journal, across the seat. "I did. Are you expecting deep, dark secrets from one night?"

He laughed. "Maybe." Ashton guided her down steps that opened into a hidden treasure. The lush greenery and flowers reminded her of Missouri Botanical Gardens.

"This is nice," she said in awe.

"My family grew up not far from here."

Lewis Park was quiet except for an occasional squeal from children on the swings. About twenty minutes into their walk, Ashton suggested they rest at a bench overlooking a small pond.

She sighed in pleasure and stretched her legs. The tranquility was relaxing. Ashton angled his body and faced her. He didn't touch her, but somehow his closeness sent goosebumps down her arms. The way his beautiful brown eyes looked at her wasn't lustful. The only way she could describe his expression was he seemed more intrigued by her.

"Now, I am really interested in your thoughts in the journal, if you want to share."

After a wonderful afternoon, it seemed silly to rehash her tirade, and she told him as much, but he persisted.

"You do know a journal is meant to be private and not shared." As she was about to pull out the pink lace-covered book with its matching pen, he stopped her. "If you don't mind, I want us to be truthful and open. I want a hint of how you think when you're angry so I won't upset you again."

He's saying the right things, Lord, pulling at my heartstrings, but is this a decoy? God didn't answer, so she went ahead and opened the journal under his watchful eye as he scooted closer.

"The first thing I wrote was 'This isn't going to work.'"

"And in bold letters." He seemed amused as he pointed to her edict.

"Yes." She faced him. "I was mad at you for standing me up."

"But I didn't. I came."

"Yes, you did," she whispered. "While I was yelling at you on paper, I was talking to God about you."

"That's good to know that you're a praying woman." He smirked.

She elbowed him. "You know that's not what I'm talking about. She scooted to create more space between them. She was becoming too comfortable with him too fast. She had to keep a clear head.

"Next." He folded his hands and looked ahead as an obedient student after being chastened for stealing a cookie or something. It was comical and a laugh-out-loud moment.

"I asked myself 'What type of relationship do you want from me? Friends or more?'"

"More." He faced her. "But being friends and brothers and sisters in Christ has to be our foundation."

"Good answer, Mr. Taylor."

"I hope it's the right answer, Sister Hayes." His eyes seemed to twinkle with mischief, and she had to grin.

Tilting her head, Dominique studied him. Despite his attire the night before, she told herself to ignore the tiredness in his eyes. Today, the freshness was there. "Do you miss church a lot?"

"It all depends on who's keeping score. I rarely miss Sundays, and I will drag myself to Bible class and sit in the back if I leave work late. As for other functions, yes, I might miss them because I'm a working man." He paused. "I've heard women like men who can keep a job, and I happen to have been at mine for thirteen years." He winked.

"Hmm." She twisted her lips, re-read one last thought, and closed the journal. "What's the most important thing to you right now?"

"After Jesus, if you let me, it would be you, hands down."

Speechless, Dominique had to turn away. This man was serious, and she wasn't ready for this, although she had convinced herself she was. He intrigued her. He seemed powerful, but acted gentle. "No further questions."

"Do you mind?" He reached for her pink pen and began to scribble his heartfelt thoughts, and soon they were communicating to each other on paper. Her personal journal no longer held her private thoughts, but his too.

Chapter 9

Since their lunch date, Ashton's attraction for Dominique was building. He wished he could see her every day, especially when he was near her address. When his eyes couldn't feast on her, his mind recaptured the brief memories they had created.

Dominique sounded amused over the phone when he teased that he had seen a woman that day who reminded him of her.

"Oh, really? And what did I look like?"

Stretching out on the sofa at his house, Ashton closed his eyes. "She was taller than you and darker skinned—"

"That doesn't sound anything like me."

Chuckling, he knew she was going to say that. "Maybe not in looks, but in her air of confidence, which triggered me to think of you."

"Good answer, Mr. Taylor."

"Well, thank you, Sister Hayes."

"Why do you always call me that when I use your surname?"

"Because even though I'm attracted to the physical and mental part of you, I can't forget about your soul. You'll always be my sister in Christ first, and it's my way of respecting you."

She was silent. He wondered what she was thinking. Finally, came her soft whisper of thanks.

"I guess I need to start being on the lookout for Brother Taylor."

He chuckled. "I'm easy to spot. Just look for one of our company trucks."

Before ending their call with a prayer, they agreed to alternate visiting each other's weekly singles meeting.

Not a day went by that Ashton didn't thank God for the blessing to his heart—Dominique.

He strolled into work on Friday morning, grinning. That day was going to be a turning point in their relationship. Dominique finally felt comfortable with letting him take the lead and pick her up for his church's sponsored movie night.

"Man, this woman has you wrapped around her finger," Marc teased him.

"A godly woman will do that to a man."

"I guess so. I've never had one, maybe that's why I'm divorced with children."

Divorce wasn't an option for Ashton. He hoped the woman he married felt the same way. Prayer would keep them together—if they stayed on their knees. He briefly thought about Joseph considering divorcing Mary, but God's spirit intervened and kept them together for His purpose. That was the type of marriage he wanted, one that was for God's purpose.

Ashton caught himself from drifting off farther. He slapped Marc on the shoulder as the man had done to him many times. "Get right with God and see what He has in store for you," he said, having the last word, then they headed in opposite directions for their trucks.

He pulled up his schedule deliveries and mentally calculated the time they would take. Ashton was confident that he would have made it to the hub by quitting time with a half hour to spare.

His morning went as planned, but his afternoon began to fall apart. Last-minute re-routed packages delayed him. He called Dominique about four. She answered with the sweetest voice.

"I'm looking forward to tonight," she said after their greeting. "As a matter of fact, I saw someone who reminded me of you."

Ashton frowned. He had very few male cousins in St. Louis, so he knew she wouldn't run into any look-alikes. "How so?"

"I was at a client's office, and this guy—almost as handsome as you—"

He snickered. She was a breath of fresh air in his life.

"He was so kind that I took notice."

"Thank you for saying that about me." He was glad she was in a good mood. "Well, your handsome man is running late. It's a good thing we're going to movie night that starts later. It's going to be tight, but I'll pick you up by seven-thirty and—"

"I'll drive," she said in a monotone. He couldn't decipher if she was upset, disappointed, or if it wasn't a big deal.

"I'm so sorry to do this to you—us—but it can't be helped."

"I understand. I'll meet you there." She said her goodbye, and Ashton was left with a sinking feeling that he had disappointed her. It couldn't be helped. The last couple hours of his shift, he had to battle against the devil, trying to put doubt in his head that he wasn't good enough to make Dominique happy.

It was a race against time when he returned to the hub at ten to six, got his vehicle and drove the half hour to his house to shower and dress. His saving grace was the film started at eight-ten. He arrived at the Regal Cinemas, then trekked across the St. Louis Outlet parking lot. Dominique was standing by the concession counter. Not good. Not only did he keep her waiting, but evidently, she had purchased her own ticket.

She stood out from others in the crowd in her two-piece light purple outfit. He didn't see any other members of his church.

This was not going as he planned, hoped, and prayed. He quickly purchased his ticket, then went inside. She didn't move as she waited for him to approach her. "I'm sorry. I'm supposed to be treating you. I see you already have the popcorn and stuff."

Her expression was unreadable, so he was clueless if she forgave him. "We'd better go and find some seats."

Ashton nodded, then lifted her popcorn tub and candy out of her arms into his. When she was about to protest, he chuckled. "I'm just carrying them, so I can hold your hand."

"Okay," she whispered as they walked into the theater. He nodded at a couple of his church members. Once they were seated, Ashton handed over her snacks and exhaled. The previews were still showing, so they hadn't missed the movie.

"I'm not going to be able to enjoy the movie if I'm not forgiven. I told you I would never cancel one of our dates." Talk to me, he willed her.

"But I thought about it."

"Ouch." Ashton hadn't thought about that. "Thank you for waiting."

She grabbed a fist full of popcorn, and stuffed it in her mouth. After Dominique swallowed, he looked at him as the light reflected off the screen. The disappointment seemed to be glaring at him. No, it was hurt.

Closing his eyes, he bowed his head and rubbed his forehead. Okay, so he messed up this time. Ashton was determined there wouldn't be another mess up as their movie started.

Dominique told herself not to be annoyed with Ashton's tardiness, but she was, and she prayed hard for God to help her. Recognizing a handful of Corinthian Church members, they offered to stay with her once she said Ashton had invited her, but was running late. She declined. There was no sense making them miss the previews, which Dominique actually liked to see, and possibly part of the movie.

This is when she missed her friend. At least if Paige had tagged along, she would have a familiar face to vent to. But Paige was attending their church's singles meeting by herself. Hopefully, Minister Ray was encouraging Paige's soul to wait on her mate while Dominique was impatiently waiting on her date.

While she wandered in front of the concession counter, she snacked on her popcorn. Of all the things to give her, Ashton gave her a journal. Did he know she would need it to vent this soon?

Stay calm, she kept telling herself. He did give her a heads up. But knowing he was on his way wasn't comforting at the moment. This was an adjustment dating a man who would miss or be late for dates.

Her building irritation imploded the moment his flustered expression came within a couple of feet in front of her. Before he said he was sorry, she could see it written all over his face. How could she be mad and happy to see him at the same time? Since she was conflicted, Dominique decided to guard her words.

As they watched the movie, she relaxed against

71

his shoulder. Besides a few chuckles, he was mostly quiet. When she glanced at him, Dominique saw the reason why. His long lashes were drifting.

Annoyance resurfaced as she recalled verse one in Ecclesiastes 3: *To everything there is a season, and a time to every purpose under the heaven.* Maybe, just maybe, her timing for dating was off. Either Ashton was the one, or she needed to wait a little longer.

Chapter 10

Not again. Ashton gritted his teeth. It was Memorial's Day weekend and he was hoping for Dominique to join him at his family barbecue. He had heard of someone's personal life interfering with a person's livelihood, but work was overstepping its boundaries in his private life.

Seasonal business peak times were predictable. Other times, it depended on the client's shipment needs. But that was the sales team to worry about. His job was just to make deliveries. His duties sounded simple enough, but it was becoming complicated. So here he was pulling into Salvation Temple's parking lot at eight-thirty and praying before he even entered the chapel that the singles meeting wasn't over yet.

God heard his prayer and granted it. However,

Dominique's minister was giving the altar call. *Perhaps I should have been more specific.* The end of the service that was most reverenced.

While members prayed, no one walked to cause a distraction for anyone contemplating their spiritual life. Those who were unsaved who wanted to give their lives to Christ, repented and took the first steps in their salvation walk—the water and spirit baptism in Jesus' name. Two men stepped into the aisle and approached the altar. Watching their submission caused the group to worship God in a thunderous praise.

Soon, Ashton was allowed to enter, and he scanned faces until he found Dominique who smiled, but didn't have the accompanying twinkle in her eyes. Paige waved.

He mouthed, *Sorry.*

Dominique nodded. He joined her as they were about to leave their offering and dismiss.

"Better late than never, Brother Taylor," Paige said.

"I hope so," he responded with his eyes on Dominique. He had never been in a dog house so many times with a woman, a woman he wanted. More than anything, he wanted to take her to dinner and make it up to her like he had when they went to lunch. Unlike his singles group at Corinthian Church, which dined out after service, Salvation Temple's members mingled afterward with light refreshments in their adjacent fellowship hall. He was grateful for her friend, Paige, who tagged along and attempted to piece together a conversation between him and Dominique.

However, her words were few.

Once they served themselves appetizers from the buffet table, they sat at an unoccupied table. Ashton gave thanks for their meal, and for the next half hour, the two of them went through the motions of enjoying each other's company, but clearly she wasn't pleased by his delay.

"My sister is barbecuing for Memorial's Day, and you're invited. I know how much you love barbecue."

"I do." She smiled. "But I'm spending the day with my parents."

He felt an invisible slap, but it caused him to flinch anyway. Dominique didn't extend an invite, and he wasn't about to intrude. Yes, he was committed to building a relationship with her, but Ashton was a hardworking man.

Like doctors who are called in for emergencies and detained to save lives, his deliveries were equally as important, possibly delivering some of the very instruments physicians needed. Most of the time, he got off of his shift after clocking in eight hours. Of all times for him not to finish deliveries on time had to be when he met Dominique. But his unpredictable schedule was part of him, and if she wanted him, she was going to have to understand.

Of course to verbalize his reasoning at the moment wouldn't go over too well. He liked Dominique. She had snagged his heart without him even knowing it, but they had to come to an understanding. *Lord, we need You if we're meant to be.*

Women. The barbecue with his family on Monday was anything but pleasant when he showed up without his date. Why did he accidentally let her name slip when he told his mother and sisters that he had met someone, so they would stop trying to set him up?

Once they had Dominique's name, age and what she did for a living, they insisted on meeting her. They had suggested the barbecue, because it would be a casual setting and there would be other guests.

Of course, it didn't matter that no one knew the cause of his and Dominique's spat. They had already judged her absence as his fault. It was his mother who pulled him aside under the guise of fixing him a to-go plate.

"What happened, son? I can tell you care about Dominique. A new relationship takes time. If you really like her, make sure she never doubts it."

Ashton glanced over his shoulder to make sure his sisters weren't close by. He peeped out the window and saw them chasing after their children.

"This is the deal: I'm a hard worker, and don't always finish my deliveries by five, but that's the exception, not the norm. My job is part of the package." He folded his arms. He knew his mother would take his side on this. His parents drilled into him the importance of a man keeping a job.

"You get no argument out of me about that, son." Wrinkles marred her flawless skin as she stared up at him, reminding him of when he used to get in trouble as a teenager.

"I've been late to a couple of our dates." The first one was a bust. He had missed it, but he wasn't about to tell his mother that.

She *tsk*ed and shook her head. "Not good. Maybe you shouldn't make any dates that you know you can't keep if you really like her as you say." With that statement, she finished wrapping his plate.

Later that night at home, Ashton gave his mother's counsel some serious thought and called Dominique. She didn't answer by the time he prepared for bed, so on his knees he prayed, "Lord, You care about the sparrows, so I know You care about me and where this relationship is headed. I'm beginning to fall in love with her, and we can use Your help."

When there was still no response from her on Tuesday morning, he sent her a text, quoting part of 1 Corinthians 13:4: *Charity suffers long, and is kind*, before he began his day. That woman knew how to twist him in knots.

At the hub, a fellow driver called in sick, so Ashton picked up some of his deliveries, which included more commercial drop-offs. It worked out, since for once in a long time, he had a light load.

He double parked at the curb at Frontenac Plaza. As he loaded up his dolly for several stores within the mall, he heard a giggle that echoed through the wind to his ears. It was a familiar, sweet sound, and he had to search out the owner. He glanced in the direction of a nearby outdoor cafe and fumbled with a couple of boxes to keep from dropping them.

Dominique was at a small table entertaining a

man. Squinting, he mustered up as much of a twenty/twenty vision as he could to get a better look. Who was he? Was this guy the reason Ashton hadn't heard from Dominique? She was stunning in red, actually, any color suited her and became his favorite. His heart dropped as it appeared they seemed to be enjoying themselves a bit too much for him.

Hurt, anger, and jealousy filled his pores. No, he was overreacting. "Lord, help me." Maybe he was being petty, and it was pure torture on his part, but Ashton took the long route to the side door into the mall. He wanted to make sure Dominique saw him.

He counted the seconds until their paths would cross. When their eyes connected, Dominique's laughter stilled, then in a flash, she dismissed him and gave her dining companion her complete attention.

That stung as Ashton's day went downhill from there. He was mad at God, the world, and Dominique. *He was done chasing Dominique Hayes.*

Chapter 11

What was Ashton's problem? Dominique wondered as she tried to mask her disappointment while wooing a client who was thinking about changing vendors for his payroll services. Too much money was on the line for her to interrupt Michael Moran's jokes to confront Ashton.

He hadn't called all weekend, and she refused to chase after men as if she were a needy woman who would accept crumbs of his time. She got more attention from men in the world. Nope, they weren't an option, so she wasn't going entertain those thoughts.

His behavior was the last straw. She was of the mind to block his number. Dominique pulled out her phone and noticed she had an old missed message and text. Both were from Ashton the previous day and early that morning. Still, she didn't bother to listen. She glimpsed his text while looking for another message from a client.

The Scripture gave her pause, but his behavior was contrary to First Corinthians 13:4. Before their last dating near-miss, they always searched for each other's qualities in a random stranger.

She couldn't help but peek at the driver when the familiar truck passed by her. It was no different when one parked at the curbside. When Ashton's face came into view, her heart fluttered like crazy. He looked so handsome, strong, and mad. *What's he doing here?* Was this a new route? Her resolve to call it quits melted away. It was revised after the look he cut her.

Trying to keep up the amused facade with her client, she smiled and nodded at appropriate times, but she was bothered by Ashton's expression and body language. Once he was inside the mall, Dominique wrapped up the lunch by asking the server for their check and arranging another meeting the following month with him along with her district manager. Her company would go to the CEO if necessary in order not to lose this account.

Mr. Moran walked her to her car, they shook hands, then parted ways. Before pulling out, she called Paige, but got her voice mail. "Call me when you get a chance."

On a business call, her friend texted back.

Paige was drumming up freelance projects here and there, so Dominique was in her corner, but still she was in a semi-crisis mode and needed   somebody to vent about her conflicting feelings.

I'm here, God whispered.

Now, she was speechless. After the Ashton sighting, her head wasn't in sync with her heart. As a matter of fact, seeing him had messed her head up. Although Dominique had planned to follow up on one of her executives' clients, she decided against it. She would work the rest of the day from home. Once there, her mind floated back to her relationship with Ashton.

It had already been a month since their awkward first date. Thinking about his somewhat "no show" at her singles meetings made Dominique tweak her determination not to settle with an ungodly man for a husband. Ashton made her realize she shouldn't settle for just *any* godly man for a mate.

It seemed as it took forever for Paige to call her back. When she did, it was to advise her she'd been tied up all day pitching her services to prospective clients.

"I don't know if my heart was better before I met Ashton or after meeting him," Dominique whined as she reflected the conversation she had over the weekend with her father. Her mother asked about the brother she mentioned she was seeing. Dominique's answers had been vague and she struggled to figure out if he'd make the cut to meet them.

Her father had huffed. *"If he can't look me in the eye and tell me man to man that he will love and honor you for the rest of his life without flinching, don't bother bringing him to my doorstep."* Byron Hayes reminded her he wouldn't easily be impressed. So at the moment, Ashton wouldn't make the cut.

"Dominique, Dominique," Paige called her name. "You're too distracted to talk to me on the phone. I'll be there within the hour."

"Okay." She disconnected, then stepped out to a small veranda, which gave her a view of the front of the house. Snuggling up in her wicker rocker, she waited for her best friend to arrive.

When Paige pulled into the driveway, Dominique waved her to the side of the house. The two hugged, and Paige joined her outside. Resting her purse, Paige stretched her legs to place her feet on a wicker ottoman. She took a deep breath, then gave Dominique her full attention. "So what happened? Where were you? What were you doing? Did he say anything?"

"I was across town schmoozing with a major client at Canyon Café. With the type of business he's giving me, I wasn't taking him to Applebee's. In my peripheral vision I saw the uniform...I took a brief glance and almost choked. Ashton seemed to have zeroed in on me. He didn't look happy, and even had the nerve to frown at me when we were within speaking distance, which of course, he did not say a word to me..."

As Dominique began to rant, Paige squeezed her lips. Clearly her friend was itching to say something. But she listened patiently until Dominique exhaled. Linking her hands, she seemed to gather her thoughts. "We're best friends, right? Sisters."

Dominique nodded.

"Good, so I can be real with you and not worry about being disowned." She paused. "Doesn't matter. Mom and Dad Hayes said I'm their second daughter anyway." Paige beamed. Their families treated each of them as part of the family.

"Why do I have a feeling I'm not going to like what you're about to say?" Dominique squinted. "Ashton and I just don't work."

"We're taught at Salvation Temple not to crave what others have, so here's the deal. We both want husbands. Ashton could or could not be the one you choose, but you have that choice. I don't. We've both talked about losing faith and hope in being gifted with a special someone. From where I'm sitting, which is on the same church pew, Ashton always shows up. Can't you work with that? That six-foot something hunk clearly has eyes for you."

"I hear you, and if this were you, I don't know if I would give you the same advice," she paused and held up a finger—"Our lives aren't fairytales. All I'm saying is show me that I'm important enough to keep his word. Don't take it for granted I'll always be there."

"You're one hundred percent right."
When Paige didn't say more, Dominique frowned. "That's it? No further convincing arguments?"

"Nope." She stood and headed to the kitchen. "All this brainstorming has got me hungry."

Paige seemed to eat anything and never gained a pound, and when Dominique was with her, she pigged out too, but would pay for it later when she got on the scale. Dominique followed her inside. "What brainstorming? We haven't reached anything definite on what I should do?"

Paige bobbed her head.

"Oh, yes you have. Ashton isn't worth taking the chance."

"Exactly." Dominique folded her arms. And there would be no kiss and makeup, since they never got around to sharing a first kiss.

Chapter 12

"This is ridiculous!" Ashton's older sister was heated at the news of the demise of his relationship with Dominique. "Why do you have a problem with commitment?"

"Me?" Ashton eyed Felicia. This was supposed to be a family dinner after church, not a tribunal on his personal business, requiring a family meeting at his sister's house.

"Yeah, you." Bailee, his baby sister, mimicked Felicia.

"One day you're in a relationship, but you somehow found yourself in some type of stalemate at the barbecue. Now a week later, you're not in a relationship. C'mon, bro." Felicia huffed. "The sisters at church don't appeal to you, and you refuse to entertain some of our girlfriends...I get that, because some aren't practicing Christians. Bailee took a chance..." She gave their younger sister a side glance. "And everything worked out with Doug. Whew. Good thing, but back to you. All of us want to see you happily married. You seemed to have liked this Dominique woman, but you deprived Bailee and me out of our sisterly rights not to meet her and give our thumbs up or down. You ain't right, bro."

Ashton rubbed his knees, ready to bolt, then he would miss out on the chicken lasagna and seven-layer salad his mother had prepared. He didn't want to verbalize what he had already rehashed in his head after seeing Dominique the week before. She hadn't responded to his call or text. Maybe he had moved too fast and was blindsided by her pretty face. He looked to his two brothers-in-law for rescue. They just shook their heads. Great, no backup.

"Dinner's warmed up," his mother yelled from the kitchen as if dinner was at her house.

"Yes." Ashton stood first. Saved by the food.

He was spared at the dinner table, but the moment they were finished eating, his sisters husbands excused themselves and took the children outside.

"Ash, you are too old to find the love of your life and let her slip away."

"I never said I was in love."

Felicia smirked. "You didn't have to. You're wearing it on that halfway good looking face of yours. If she is all that, then fight to make her understand why you've been a jerk. Then we need to meet her to cast our votes."

"Excuse me?" He blinked. This was the very reason why he tried to keep his private life secret—his sisters were too opinionated about his choices. He recalled at least two sisters at their church Felicia felt didn't make the cut.

"Listen, I can't help you if you don't tell me what's wrong." She frowned.

"I don't recall asking for help," Ashton countered.

"Not in so many words, but seriously, talk to us. We love you," Felicia said in a soft tone that reflected her sincerity.

The love part did him in. There was no denying his sisters had his back. Her expression made him spill his guts about showing up late for dates, then seeing Dominique with another guy.

"All I have to say is you are so wrong for skipping out on those dates." Bailee *hmph*ed and folded her arms.

"I second that," Felicia added before Ashton could reiterate he didn't stand Dominique up. "She probably doesn't think you're serious about her. And you said, she's a big-shot manager. As far as after the guy, it was probably a business meeting unless they were holding hands and nibbling on each other's lips.

Ashton couldn't tame his nostrils from flaring. Nobody better not kiss her before he does! He balled his fist in irritation. What was the message earlier at church? Ecclesiastes 7:9: *"Be not hasty in thy spirit to be angry: for anger rests in the bosom of fools."* On that text, their pastor preached for a lengthy time that God doesn't suffer fools. Ashton took a deep breath to regain control of his senses. "I am—I mean was—

serious about a relationship with her," he defended with a soft answer as Pastor Garmany quoted Proverbs 15:1: *"A soft answer turns away wrath: but grievous words stir up anger,"* before concluding his sermon

"Great. Now, prove it. When is the last time you've given her flowers?" Bailee lifted an eyebrow.

"It seems like I've opened an account at Miss Nancy's flower shop." Although in reality, it had only been twice and he paid for both.

"Uncle Ash, see Elmo?" three-year-old Stephan asked, rushing into the house. The boy might be his nephew, but he was a carbon copy of Ashton when he was a boy.

"Sure, buddy," Ashton said as the child ran away to get what Ashton thought would be a stuffed toy, but returned with a furry puppy. "When did you get a pet?" He rubbed the dog's head. "Elmo?"

"Yesterday," Felicia said as her two-year-old daughter scrambled to her mother. "We're getting a kitty."

"Really?" Ashton lifted his brow at his sister. "You're going to have a regular animal kingdom."

Felicia laughed. "We grew up with pets. Alex and I don't have a problem. Maybe you should give Dominique a dog."

"Right." He grunted. "Flowers you only have to water. A dog, you have to feed, walk, and clean up poop."

"But who can resist those puppy eyes?" He and Felicia stared at Elmo as the dog blinked at them. You can borrow mine."

"You're serious, aren't you?"

"Hey, if she's a dog lover like most women are, then it would definitely be a conversation starter. And you two may need to start from the beginning."

Ashton couldn't believe he was actually considering her offer.

"You've until Stephan's bed time, then he'll be coming for you on his tricycle." Felicia smirked and gathered Elmo, his food, toys, and sleeping blanket. "If Elmo doesn't win her over, take your niece and nephew. They'll have her wrapped around their fingers."

"Ain't no way." Ashton considered himself a good uncle, but a babysitter, he was not, so he took the leash. If the puppy didn't work, then he would go to Plan C, which he hadn't figured out yet. "Bye, Felicia."

A few hours later, he parked in front of Dominique's house with Elmo in his travel cage. Getting out of his car, he put Elmo on a leash and stared at the bungalow. On the drive over, he realized they needed to compromise, but how?

He exhaled, doubting an animal could mend fences. "Here goes." Instead of ringing her doorbell, he leaned up against his car and tapped her name on his phone. Would she answer when she recognized his number? She did, and her voice warmed his heart. "Can you come out and play?"

"What?"

"Look out your window."

Seconds later, her front door opened. They both were still on the phone. He watched her expression. *Elmo, work your charm, buddy*, as the puppy wagged his tail.

Instantly ignoring him, he watched as she strolled down her driveway and headed for the puppy, Dominique squatted, rubbed the puppy's head, and gave the animal the attention Ashton wanted.

"Hey, girl. What's her name?" she asked without looking up at him.

"It's a he. Elmo."

"Elmo?" She stood and he continued to feast on her beauty. Dressed up, or down in jeans and a long sleeved green top, she never looked better to him.

He chuckled first at her amused expression, then she laughed. It felt good to see her smile. He missed her. "My three-year-old nephew named him." He stepped closer. "I'm sorry. I borrowed the dog to get me out of your doghouse. The pun is intended."

Her stare was intense as she jutted her chin. One hand went to her hip. She twisted her lips as she squinted. Seemingly coming to a decision, she dropped her arm and began to retreat to her house.

"What, it didn't work?" His shoulders slumped. Dominique twirled around when she got to the door. "Let me get my keys so we can take him for a walk."

Ashton couldn't stop the grin from stretching across his face. He picked up the dog and rubbed his head. "I owe you big time, buddy. You'll get a top-of-the-line doghouse for Christmas."

Chapter 13

Humbleness was the foundation of Dominique's Christian walk, but her proud spirit had caused her internal torture. With so many Scriptures on pride, James 4:6—*God resists the proud, but gives grace unto the humble*—gave her pause to reflect.

When Ashton called, her heart swelled at the deep timbre of his voice. When she opened the door and saw him, her heart flipped, her eyes danced for joy, and his presence quenched a thirst her mouth suddenly had. With all that rejoicing going on, Dominique repented for her foolish behavior.

The puppy was cute, but Ashton was cuter, leaning against his shiny car as if he was posing for a photo shoot. His biceps bulged under the polo shirt. He looked handsome, strong, and perhaps vulnerable.

She wanted to run into his arms and hug him so tight that he would lose consciousness, but they needed to come to an understanding.

"I'm so sorry…" Ashton said. "The way I behaved when I saw you at lunch. When you didn't return my call and text, I assumed the joker was stealing away my heart." He fingered her chin. "You." His apology had been the true act of humility—at least that's what her pastor taught. If they couldn't tell one another sorry, how could they tell God sorry?

"Me too." She needed to create some distance between them to think clearly. Otherwise she would fall into his arms and kiss him like a woman out of control. Refocusing, she explained, "The joker was a big client—big. He was considering going with our competitor for his payroll solution. I'll treat him to lunch every week to keep his business." She jutted her chin.

Staring, Ashton nodded, but said nothing while Elmo ran circles around their feet. "Since we haven't spoken, I've seemed to see you in people every day—in their smiles, laugh, and walk, which made me miss you."

When the dog pulled on the leash, Ashton untangled them and continued their stroll. He also linked his fingers through hers. "Basically, standing you up breaks my heart too. I never realized dating could be so challenging when I haven't put my priorities in order."

He was just realizing that? Smirking, Dominique held her peace instead of rubbing it in.

"A very wise woman told me not to plan a date

with you I couldn't keep."

"Sounds like something a mom would say." When he affirmed that, Dominique slowed her steps and looked away. "For me, the perfect date is at a place where we can share what we have in common, which is the Lord."

"And that's what makes you so attractive—your love for God. I've never wanted a woman as much as you, so at times I've tried to pull off the impossible at work. I can't do it, babe."

She liked the sound of the endearment on his lips. And the honesty shining from his brown eyes.

"God is my witness that from this day forward, I'll be careful what I promise you, so that I will keep them." He leaned forward and kissed her forehead, then brought her hand to his lips as she shivered from his touch.

In a daze, Dominique watched him as he placed her hand on his heart. The beat was strong. She knew what was coming next, and her lids fluttered. Elmo started to yelp for attention, but Ashton didn't stop from delivering their first sweet kiss.

"I love you," he whispered against her lips as they slowly parted too soon. "I don't need a year to figure that out. My heart knew in weeks."

"I love you." She pecked soft kisses on his lips until he begged her to stop. She giggled.

Retaking her hand in his, he tugged her toward a nearby bench, pausing for Elmo to take a potty break.

After they took a seat, she wrapped her arm through his, and rested her head on his shoulder. Dominique was content to say nothing as she closed her eyes. She had finally found a man to love, but it wasn't without challenges and she wasn't sure how they would resolve them. But with Jesus, all things were possible. "Thank You, Lord."

Ashton chuckled. "I just gave thanks myself." He kissed the top of her head, and the sensation of his touch seemed to spread from the point of contact.

So this was how temptation felt. Opening her eyes, she reached down and picked up the puppy and began to cuddle it for a distraction. "Quote me a scripture."

"*'Surely goodness and mercy shall follow me all the days of my life, and I—we—shall dwell in the house of the Lord forever,'*" he said without hesitation.

"Psalm 23."

"That's one Scripture that came to mind. It's too soon to quote another one."

Biting her lips, Dominique wondered if it was Proverbs 18:22: *Whoso finds a wife finds a good thing, and obtains favor of the LORD.* That was the only one that mattered to a single woman, at least her and Paige.

He continued, "I thought about God's favor on my life, which seems to have followed me since I made up my mind to follow Christ as a teenager."

"Amen."

"So are we good, Sister Hayes?"

Angling her body, she looked into his eyes. "More than good, Brother Taylor." He kissed her forehead.

She closed her eyes, hoping for a repeat of the

earlier ritual when she received his kiss on her lips, but he stopped there.

"Since I'm out the doghouse, now I can return Elmo to my sister's house. Of course, I need you to tag along as evidence that I've mended my ways."

Dominique normally would have said no since she wasn't presentable to meet a family member, but with their apologies, things were changing...and they were a team. Plus, Ashton's puppy-dog expression overpowered her. "Sure."

All things work together for the good to those who love the Lord and are called according to His purpose. Romans 8:28 never sounded so good to Ashton's ears now that he and Dominique had kissed and made up. Although the makeup part was enjoyable, he didn't want to go through another misunderstanding like that again. Hearing her voice had become part of his daily routine that he didn't want to break. The man in him wanted to indulge in their kiss until his heart's content, but the spiritual pulled the reins.

With Dominique in the passenger seat and Elmo inside his cage in the back, Ashton drove to his sister's house feeling like a different man. Now, he understood the old saying, "my better half." Dominique's presence calmed him.

"I never want to make you think you're not

important. I know I have to make some changes at work," he admitted as he neared Felicia's.

"Thank you," she whispered, fumbling with her fingers without glancing his way. "I wasn't sure where I stood with you, but I'm going to ask God to work on me because if a man is willing to work hard—" she faced him—"I don't want to be the cause of that man's unemployment."

He shook his head. That would never happen, him jeopardizing his job. "I need to learn how to balance my life between work and personal." He paused. "After kissing you today, whew!" He glanced and caught a glimpse of a blush. "We're going to have to stay prayerful that our attraction doesn't put God to shame because we've sinned."

She agreed as Ashton arrived at his sister's house as the sun was setting. He helped Dominique out of the car, then grabbed Elmo's cage and supplies. Squeezing her hand, he looked up. "Isn't the sky beautiful?"

"Yes."

"I want us to be able to share the simple things of life in addition to the pampering I plan for you."

Shrugging, she had a teasing glint in her eyes. "Who am I to keep you from spoiling me? I approve this message." She giggled, and he fell in love with her all over again.

In sync, they climbed the stairs to the porch. He *shh*ed her as he gently nudged her to move to the side out of view before he rang the doorbell.

Felicia opened the door. Her eyes widened in surprise. "You're back already? That's good for

Stephan who has been worrying about his Elmo. I'm sorry, little brother, she didn't forgive you."

"But I did." Dominique came to his aid, stepping into Felicia's view.

His sister screamed, then covered her mouth, probably as not to wake the children. "Dominique. Lord, thank You!" She waved her hand in the air. "You're beautiful. Thank you for having mercy on my knuckleheaded brother." She stepped out on the porch and hugged Dominique. "Girl, we have a lot to talk about. Come on inside," Felicia said, pushing Ashton and the dog aside.

Ashton intercepted and wrapped his arm around Dominique's tiny waist. "Not so fast. This is the only delivery today." He handed over the cage. "Thanks, buddy. Remember what I said about your Christmas present." The puppy whined and wagged his tail.

Once they were back in the car, he faced Dominique. "I know I was probably wrong for that, but can't a man in love be selfish?"

She winked. "This time only."

He brought her hand to his lips. "If you're game, let's have a surprise date night during the week since the workload varies from day to day. I don't want to wait until the weekend to see you."

Her eyes sparkled. "I guess when I wake up in the morning, I'll have something to look forward to."

That week, Tuesday was date night. When an outdoor concert he wanted them to attend was rained out, she suggested sitting on her covered veranda, watching the rain and reading their Bibles.

He let her pick her favorite book of the Bible. She

chose Jude. With only one chapter and twenty-five verses, they were able to exchange their thoughts and how it applied to their lives.

"I'm happy," Dominique said out of nowhere. She patted her chest. "With you I'm in a perfect place."

Ashton choked at her admission. "Being with you, babe, reading our Bibles is like food to my soul." He placed his hand over his heart.

They weren't in a rush to feast on a light dinner of sandwiches and salads she had prepared. They sat quietly, holding hands.

A few hours later, they called it a night with a soft kiss and tight hug. Driving back home across town, Ashton grinned. A man who thought a woman's body was sexy hadn't met a godly woman. Dominique was sexy, and it came from her soul.

Two weeks had passed since they had reconciled and Ashton was proud to say he made it to one of Dominique's singles meetings on time. It was a perfect date when he picked up her and they arrived at Salvation Temple together. After service, he treated her and Paige to a late snack instead of indulging at their church's fellowship hall with the other members.

That night, Minister Ray moderated a panel discussion where brothers and sisters asked and answered honestly questions about expectations when dating.

He had squeezed Dominique's hand when one sister stated, "I have to know I'm special and not just another sister on a list for dinner before moving on."

Inwardly, Ashton was glad that they had resolved that issue in their relationship.

When the Fourth of July rolled around, he accompanied Dominique to her parents' house for a barbecue and a formal introduction. Mr. Hayes shook his hand, then twisted his lips as he sized Ashton up.

"Have a seat," her father had said, then reached for his electronic tablet. He tapped on the screen, and seconds later, his questions began and evidently, Ashton's answers were documented. The interrogation was nothing short of forty-five minutes, and Ashton politely subjected himself to the scrutiny.

"That's it for now," Mr. Hayes said, about to shut down his device, but Ashton stopped him.

"Please make sure you put in all caps that I love your daughter."

Mr. Hayes grunted with a crocked smile. "Like they say in Missouri, 'I'm from the Show-me-State, and you'll have to show me'. I think your signature will be required on this."

What! Ashton kept his eyes from bulging. Accepting the challenge, Ashton grinned. "Do you have a stylus?"

Chapter 14

At times, Dominique felt guilty about her bliss with Ashton when Paige was still waiting for her special someone, plus steady employment at a company that was willing to pay what her friend was worth.

Like sisters, they had always looked out for each other, so it wasn't surprising Paige tried to minimize their get-togethers to give Dominique and Ashton space for date nights. Dominique was not okay with that, so she insisted her friend tag along on outings with Ashton that weren't meant for two.

For the most part, Paige declined their invitations, but couldn't resist the highlights from a new Japanese paintings and calligraphy exhibit at the St. Louis Art Museum, since she had completed numerous designer projects that called for cultural themes.

Ashton was never far away as she and Paige scrutinized different pieces on display. She loved him even more giving her bonding time with her best friend. It didn't go unnoticed by Paige that Ashton wasn't demanding for attention.

The following Friday, she and Paige were lounging in Dominique's living room, waiting for Ashton to pick them up for a singles event at his church. "Ashton may deliver packages, but the man is a package deal. So do you think he was worth the wait?"

"Yes." Dominique didn't have to think about it. "I'll admit I was delusional about our relationship. I guess I thought being with the right one meant everything would be perfect, free of trials." She chuckled. "Sounds silly that I would think Satan would let me enjoy God's blessings without some sort of sabotage on his part. I'm so glad you were praying for me and Ashton."

Paige nodded. "We've always been each other's cheerleaders in crisis. You used your connections to get me in on the bidding for projects. I appreciate you too." She exhaled. "I just would like to have a steady job when I meet the right one, so it would look like I've got myself together."

"That makes no sense." Dominique rolled her eyes. "It's not like you're going to be paying for the dates." When Paige didn't appeared convinced, Dominique added, "Well, Minister Ray said to pray for our future husbands. Let's add a footnote that he has a good job."

"That's a double Amen from me." She grinned. They slapped a high five as Dominique's doorbell rang.

Ashton arrived with a bouquet of flowers for her and a rose for Paige. She mouthed her thank you to him for thinking of Paige. Her love for the man was swelling more about each day.

"Okay, ladies, grab your Bibles and let's go play some trivia at my church. I hope the two Salvation Temple ladies I'm bringing can keep up." He winked, and she and Paige cut him a side glance before laughing.

Once at his church, Ashton was adamant about Paige being on their team. He also chose two single brothers to round out the group of five players.

As Dominique scanned the room, she wondered and then prayed that Paige would walk away with a special prize—winning some godly man's heart. Paige didn't, but despite their team losing by four points, they all had a good time. Dominique was even surprised by Ashton's competitive spirit.

Before summer came to an end, she and Ashton took sailing lessons at Creve Coeur Lake in suburban St. Louis County and went on a few double dates with members from their churches.

Now, when she attended the singles meeting at her church, it was no big deal, because she knew Ashton's heart was with her even when he wasn't. By the end of the summer, they had a big celebration.

"It seemed like it took forever, but God is faithful!" Paige lifted her glass of lemonade in a toast. Paige's family, Dominique, and Ashton were there to click their glasses with her. "Finally, a job!" She danced in her chair with excitement.

"Now, if we can get you a nice young brother in the Lord like Dominique," Mom. Blake said as Paige's brothers groaned.

"There's no rush," Benjamin, the oldest at thirty-eight said.

The good-natured scolding started as Ashton reached across the table and squeezed her hand. It didn't go unnoticed by Mom Blake.

A week later, Dominique's parents accepted an invitation to celebrate Labor Day at Ashton's mother's house.

"You think he's going to propose in front of family?" Dominique asked as she changed her dress twice and shoes four times under Paige's watchful eye. Now that her friend was gainfully employed, they decided to celebrate with the two of them taking a trip to Spain next summer, so Paige could get back on her feet solo again.

"If he does, he'll be standing at the altar with a broken leg for leaving me out of the loop." Her friend scowled and the expression was comical.

Dominique giggled until she released a hearty laugh.

"I'm half serious." Paige added, "The other half of me will be rejoicing for you. That would be a memorable way to end your summer with an engagement. But even if he doesn't propose, I still think it's sweet for couples' parents to get together. Maybe if more families were more involved in a positive way for couples, there might be less in-law problems."

Dominique agreed. "You know of all the dates we had this summer, I really cherish the ones where we studied our Bible together. Not only did those times bring us closer to each other, but closer to the Lord Jesus too. God's ways are perfect, and I have a better appreciation for James 1:4: *Let patience have her perfect work, that ye may be perfect and entire, wanting nothing.*"

"Hmm. I'd say we've been more impatient than patient."

"Yeah, but through the patience we did have, God perfected it and gave me the perfect man."

Ashton had been thinking about marriage a lot lately. There was no doubt he wanted to spend the rest of his life with Dominique, but could he be all she wanted in a husband? Actually, off and on since early September, then through October.

Now, it was November, A man practicing godly abstinence could only hold off so long. But questions arose: was he positively sure? Would he make a good husband? Would his job interfere with family time? So when his heart was in turmoil, Jesus calmed it through prayer.

"You're so easy to please, you know that?" Ashton said, towering over Dominique as she stepped back to let him enter.

She stood on her tiptoes to receive his kiss, and he didn't disappoint. Once Dominique closed the door, she took the bag of goodies. "Loving you is easy."

She was rewarded with another kiss. Guiding him into the kitchen, she prepared a pot of chili. "Thanks for the coloring books."

"Anything for you, babe."

She scooped them both bowls of chili, he asked for the blessing of their food, then dug in. "You're a great cook, you know that?"

She blushed from his compliments on the simplest things. "Do you know we've been dating for five months?"

"Yep, on Thursday," he said and stuffed another spoonful into his mouth.

Surprised, her heart fluttered. "I can't believe you know the exact date. I was rounding it off."

He shook his head. "How can I ever forget the first day I saw you? I believe the matchmaking began in heaven that day, so that's where I'm beginning my count."

Tilting her head, she stared at him in awe. "I love the man you have let God make of you."

He stopped eating and leaned forward. "I'm glad God knows best and has given me a virtuous woman."

That's the way things had developed between

them. Not a moment went by without a compliment and her feeling she was cherished.

After they ate, he cleared the table and loaded the dishwasher as she pulled the adult coloring books out of the bag. It was a hobby they stumbled across during the summer and found it not only relaxing, but an enjoyable activity for them to do together.

She chose the one with inspirational quotes. Once he joined her at the table, they reached for coloring pencils and began.

"Can you believe the year is almost over?" she said as she stayed inside the bold lines.

"Yes. I can't wait to experience each season with you." He winked.

"I can't wait to share our holiday traditions with you, our family recipes on Thanksgiving and we do Christmas community services." She got excited just thinking about it.

"Babe." He wrapped his strong hands around hers. "The holidays are peak seasons for Package Express. I may be missing in action for some of those activities, especially next month."

"Wow." Dominique bowed her head to blink back the disappointment. With her family, the holidays were her favorite time of year. Behind closed doors, her heart was heavy without that special person to create those special memories. She thought she would finally have that this year with Ashton.

"Hey," Ashton whispered. He rubbed his thumbs against her hands. "Baby, we'll have as many date nights as we can get in. As a matter of fact, I noticed your leaves are starting to fall. We can work out together and rake them on Saturday, then go to a jazz concert or something that night, if you want."

Dominique's heart warmed at the same time she realized she had a last-minute commitment. "That's sweet, but lawn maintenance is included in my association fees. Plus, I forgot to tell you I have a weekend conference to attend in Denver. I leave on Friday. I'm sorry." It looked like his heart dropped. She reached out and rubbed his beard.

He exhaled. "That's okay. Maybe the following weekend."

"Sorry, every fall my mother's Living Victorious Association has it's annual ladies' weekend retreat. Paige and I have been going with our mothers," she paused, "for years, as long as I can remember."

He huffed. "Dare I ask if you have any other dates available this month?"

"Let me check my calendar." She laughed, but he didn't.

He didn't say anything as he picked up the pencil and began to color. He shook his head. "I never imagined you working on the weekends. Would it sound bad for me to say that's our time?"

"I recall saying the same thing in the beginning about our Friday night single meetings."

He gently cupped her cheeks. "We'll survive this, because I want a lifetime with you."

Dominique was in a daze, mesmerized by his warm brown eyes, until her head shouted, "Hey! Rewind his words." So she blinked. "A lifetime? What are you saying?"

"That I love you, and I want us to talk about the next step in our relationship." He leaned his forehead against hers.

Her heart danced in her chest as she frowned. "Are you proposing?"

"If I knew we both were sure we're ready. We need to pray, fast, and seek God's timing."

She had been ready for years.

Chapter 15

Ashton was determined to romance Dominique, even during peak season. Whenever he had deliveries for Miss Nancy's flower shop, he would make a quick stop at her house and leave her flowers, whether she had a delivery or not. Today, Dominique did.

He parked in front of her condo, and trekked up her driveway with a small bouquet of flowers and her small packages. Ashton got a surprise when she opened the door. "Well, hello, ma'am," he greeted. He seldom saw her in suits, but she was just as stunning as when she wore jeans. "You have a delivery." He tried to sound professional and they both laughed. "Is everything okay? You didn't tell me you were working from home?"

"I can't tell you all my secrets. Anyway, when I was notified of the date of my delivery, I decided to work half a day from home so I could be here to give you this, then I'm heading out." She grinned, presenting him with a sack and a cup of hot chocolate. "For you to stay warm."

The woman knew how to humble him. "Baby," he said, "I got this for you." They made the exchange, then he leaned in and kissed her. "Thanks, babe, but I've got to go. Heavy load today." He reluctantly turned back to the truck. The warm cup in his hand reminded him of the chilly wind.

"Love you," Dominique called from inside the doorway.

"Love you back, baby," he said, climbing inside his truck. Before he pulled off, he heard her yell something about placing orders just to see him.

He chuckled, gave thanks for his meal, then took a sip from the cup. He didn't have any problems being her deliveryman, considering they had gone two straight weeks without any surprise date nights because of work. But Dominique seemed to make good on her promise to order more things, because when he did make her deliveries, not only was she there to receive them, but always had something hot for him to eat.

"We're a team," she had said.

On Thanksgiving, Dominique attended church with him followed by brunch at his mother's house. His mother loved her, and his sisters seemed to be in awe of her personal accomplishments. Even Elmo seemed glad to see her.

He chuckled as he watched and stuffed his mouth with a second helping of eggs before Dominique returned to her seat and playfully punched him in the shoulder. "Hey, save some room for my parents' house."

"Trust me. I always have room." He winked and kept eating.

A few hours later, Ashton was at the table again at the Hayes' house, devouring her mother's special blend of dressing with apple bits.

For some reason, her parents were fascinated by his deliveries this time of year. "Although Amazon is starting to move into the delivery business, we and other shipping companies still have the bulk of the deliveries, beginning tomorrow until Christmas Eve."

"That sounds like long days." Mr. Hayes seemed to have sympathy for him.

"It is, even with the drivers' helpers. We're a society of online shoppers for everything from sewing notions to toasters to an eighty-five inch smart television."

"So who are your helpers?" Dominique asked, snuggling up to him under the watchful eye of her parents. Mrs. Hayes smiled, Mr. Hayes frowned.

"High school seniors, part-timers, anyone who wants to make extra money for the holidays for a few weeks," he explained, which is why I unfortunately need to call it a night and take my beautiful lady home. Since I'm not on vacation, I'll have a long day ahead of me tomorrow." He looked into her eyes, then lifted her hand to his lips where he brushed a kiss on it. She shivered, her mother sighed and Mr. Hayes cleared his throat.

Somehow, the first chance he got, Ashton was going to talk to her father about marrying his daughter.

After they said their goodbyes, Ashton took Dominique home. He delivered a sweet kiss to her lips, and she delivered a plan that didn't sit well in his guts.

"You're what?" Ashton roared, startling Dominique, then taming his reaction and apologizing. "Babe, I don't think that's a good idea."

"Listening to you, I want to experience what it's like to be in your shoes. While most of us are taking vacations, including me, you'll be working like a dog." She folded her arms. "We're a team, remember?"

"Not this type of teamwork. Plus, you probably make more money in one day with Global Payroll Solutions than what our helpers will make in a week," he tried to reason with her. He twisted his lips. "We work our drivers' helpers to the bone. This is no place for my sweet little lady."

"Don't let my heels and makeup fool you. I was a tomboy growing up." She jutted her chin.

Her defiant expression wasn't amusing as he rubbed his neck in frustration, but Ashton dared not laugh. *Dominique has no idea what she signed up for.*

"Ash," she smiled. "It's not about the money, it's about being with you while I'm on vacation."

His woman was missing the point. "What about Paige? Don't you two have something planned? And most certainly you'll miss your singles meetings."

"Paige will understand, and as long as I don't miss Sunday service, I'll be okay." She had the final word when she gave him a hug and nudged him out of her doorway. "Now, go home. You'll need your rest.

Tomorrow is going to be a long day."

"And a long night, praying she would change her mind," Ashton mumbled as he got back into his car and drove away. First thing in the morning, he would alert human resources to be on the lookout for an application from Dominique, if indeed she made good and applied. If somehow, she got hired, he would request her on his route. Just knowing she might go through with this would cause him a restless night.

Chapter 16

Dominique had waited three days before someone from Package Express called her about interviewing for a driver's helper position. She was so giddy with excitement, she called Paige. "Do you think they'll hire me?"

"I'm surprised they called you once they looked over your resume."

Sipping her morning brew, Dominique thought so too. "It was a short application. I go in this afternoon for an interview."

"When do you plan to tell Mr. Taylor?"

"After I'm hired, of course." She laughed. "We've talked about marriage a couple of times, and this is a good way for me to put myself in his shoes."

"Hmm-mmm. Okay, I've got to get back   to

work." Paige sighed. "Sounds so good to say, work."

Dominique agreed and they disconnected. She wondered if Ashton had something to do with her getting an interview. Neither one of them discussed the topic since Thanksgiving. If she got hired, it would be an adventure for both of them.

Fifteen minutes before her scheduled interview, Dominique pulled into the assigned space for visitors at Package Express. Instead of a power suit, she dressed down in a simple white blouse and dress slacks.

She met with an older woman, Mrs. Oldham, and despite the woman's friendly demeanor, it was a hard sell to convince the woman she really wanted the job. "Every year, my family performs community service for the holiday." She went on to explain who could benefit from the proceeds, then thanked her.

Dominique walked out of the interview in disbelief. She could convince clients to trust her company with their billion dollar payroll, yet she couldn't persuade this woman to hire her for a nine dollar and fifty cent an hour job. She shrugged as she got into her car and drove on. At least she tried.

She had barely walked into her house when Mrs. Oldham called, and offered her the job. "Can you start tomorrow morning?"

"Absolutely," Dominique answered, eyeing the time and hoping she had time to get her hair and nails done.

"I'll email you your tax forms to sign and a safety manual for you to review ASAP. The driver will call in the morning and advise where you will meet him.

He will have a uniform for you to wear and document your start and end time."

Driver? She frowned. The only driver she wanted to work with was Ashton. She gnawed on her lips after the call ended. What if she got stuck with a mean and rude driver? Dominique would quit in a minute.

Now she wondered if she should let Ashton know. She sent him a text: It's official. I'm a driver's helper for peak season.

While waiting to hear from him, Dominique called her stylist to get a last minute appointment. Too bad Paige was working, because she could treat her to a manicure.

"If you can get here within the hour, I can always squeeze in my best client," Brenda "Bunnie" Ferguson said. "But you just were in here last week. What's the occasion?"

"I'll tell you when I get there," she disconnected as a text came in from Ashton. Although I'm not happy about it, I love you and I have your back.

Thank you, she texted back.

She changed and headed to Love Your Hair Salon. While Bunnie was finishing a box braid updo, Dominique decided to get a last minute facial.

"Okay, what's the special occasion," Bunnie asked once Dominique was seated in her stylist chair.

"I got a new gig as a driver's helper and I want to look my best." She smiled.

Bunnie spun her chair around. "What? Did you lose that big-time job?"

"Oh no. I'm on vacation, so I thought it would be

fun to work alongside my boyfriend, and I want to look my best. Remember, I told you he's a driver."

"I could think of other ways to spend quality time with a man. Working, isn't one of them." She massaged Dominique's scalp. "Your hair is really growing since I switched to those new products. Do you want to let it grow out for the winter?"

Dominique decided against it. Ashton always complimented her short style. "Nope. Trim it, please." Once, Bunnie finished, she sat at Mitzi's station for a manicure.

She didn't hear from Ashton until late that night after she had climbed in bed.

"Hey, baby. Sorry to wake you," his voice sounded tired.

"I told you. I can sleep better after hearing your voice." She snuggled deeper under the covers.

"And you're going to need your rest. I'm your driver, and you don't have to meet me at a random location, since you're in my territory. I also have a uniform for you. It's the smallest size human resources had."

"Thank you for letting me be your helper."

There was silence before he replied with, "I had to keep you out of trouble. Be prepared for hard work." He said a brief prayer, then ended the call with his profession of love.

Early the next morning, Dominique prayed and read her Bible before checking her emails. Although she was on vacation, she answered those marked urgent. Next, she showered, applied her makeup, and threw on her sweats, waiting for Ashton to bring her uniform. When she saw his truck, she opened her before he had got out of his truck.

"This is so exciting!"

He lifted an eyebrow, and handed over her clothes. "Since I'm on the clock, I need to remain with my truck."

"Okay." She hurried and changed. She wasn't used to this matter-of-fact side of her boyfriend. In record time, she was dressed in Package Express attire from the pants, shirt, skull cap, and jacket. She smiled at her reflection.

She locked up and hurried outside to Ashton who was waiting to assist her up into his truck. "You, by far, are the prettiest helper."

"Thanks. Before I get in, I want to take a selfie of us."

He groaned. "Sure, babe. But we need to get going if we want to finish before midnight."

"Midnight?" Horror washed over her face. "You're kidding, right."

He didn't answer. Once she was strapped in, Dominique felt like she was ten feet in the air. Batting her eyes, she grinned at him. "Reporting to work, boss." She gave him a salute.

"Did you read the safety manual?"

"Before I went to bed." Dominique nodded.

"Good. Now, this is the way we're going to work this. When I pull up to a block and there are multiple drop-offs, I'll give you the smaller packages and you deliver to those addresses, and I'll take the heavier loads."

"Sounds like a plan," she said then chatted about

their first Christmas together. She was impressed with how he handled the big truck like it was a sports car.

Turning on Pinehurst Circle, Ashton parked midway down the street and unbuckled his seatbelt. "Let's go," he said, then added, "sweetheart."

"Okay." She smiled and leaned in for a kiss, and he delivered. Next, he helped her down, and she trailed him to the back of the truck.

Dominique sucked in her breath when Ashton opened the door and boxes were stacked up from top to bottom and left to right. She swallowed. *Lord, please don't let this take until midnight.*

Ashton shifted and grabbed boxes as if they were building blocks. He placed two in her arms—one didn't look that small to her.

"These go to 1494." He pointed, then heaved the larger boxes in his arms and jogged across the street.

She huffed, then performed her task. She would need to spend more hours on the treadmill to keep this up. By the six or seventh delivery, Dominique was getting nauseous from the stop and go, but she didn't dare to complain. One thing she looked forward to was the soft kiss they shared before getting out. Despite the number of boxes they had delivered, his truck was like a tunnel and there was no sliver of light. Now, she understood why Ashton was late to dates. Actually, she was surprised he even made it, judging from this load. Never again would she give him a hard time about working late.

The good news, Dominique had learned the routine and didn't wait for him to put the packages in her arms. She swiped them for herself, checked the addresses and raced across the lawn of a house that was well lit from the outside, because it was almost dark at five o'clock and they were still on the job.

She rang the bell as Ashton had instructed her. The door opened immediately, and she came face to face with her district manager as she was about to say, "Merry Christmas."

"Dominique?"

She smiled. "Hi, Mr. Jeffries." Did he live there? The package was addressed Tiffany Love.

"Why are you delivering packages? Surely, you don't need this chicken scratch." He frowned and his expression indicated he was waiting for an answer, but so was Ashton in the truck. Upper-level managers were well paid, and it was assumed they didn't need a second job.

When she saw Ashton jump in the truck and rev up the engine, she made her escape. "Sorry. Got to go. We have a lot of packages left. Oh, and I am on vacation." She waved and raced back to the truck. The front door to the house didn't close as her boss's boss stared after her.

She strapped in, wishing Ashton would pull off.

"Hey, is everything okay? I was about to rescue you."

"That would have been nice," she mumbled to herself, but loud enough for him to hear.

Ashton circled the cul-de-sac and drove past the house where Mr. Jeffries remained in the doorway. "Was he flirting or giving you a hard time about the late delivery?"

"That was my district manager."

When she decided to do this, Dominique didn't realize that she might deliver boxes to people she knew.

"I'm sure he didn't expect to see you." Ashton chuckled.

"Yep, you're right." And he didn't look happy, Dominique didn't say. Even though she was with Ashton, the job was no longer fun. She was ready to go home.

Ashton couldn't wait for the night to be over. He loved Dominique and cherished every moment they spent together, but she only slowed him down First, she was too prissy to do this type of work. She wore the uniform, but couldn't do the job. She messed up his work flow when she leaned in for a kiss before disembarking his truck. That was the worker side of him.

But the man who loved her appreciated her presence, perfume and melodious laugh. Dominique definitely added a woman's touch to his shift with her thoughtfulness, packing a meal for them. Otherwise, they would have had another delay to eat.

What concerned him now was her mood changed after coming face-to-face with a big boss. What happened? Was she in trouble? She didn't offer an explanation, and he didn't pry. He had to stay focused on his deliveries. It was seven-thirty, and they still had about fifty boxes on the truck and twelve more stops. Besides using the restroom facilities at a gas station, they had been working hard.

As the silence stretched between, Ashton was surprised to see the quietness had lulled her to sleep as exhaustion appeared to overpower her.

He kissed her forehead, but didn't disturb her for the rest of the evening. One thing was for sure, another driver wouldn't had been easy on her, despite her beauty.

She wasn't meant for this blue-collar work, just like he wasn't comfortable in an executive office setting.

At ten o'clock, he rolled up in front of her house. She didn't wake. The moon cast a soft light on her face. His Sleeping Beauty looked like she was in her deep sleep. After turning off the engine, he unstrapped his belt, got out and walked around to her door.

He released her seatbelt constraints, then lifted her petite body in his arms. She snuggled closer and smiled. Ashton grabbed her purse and lunch sack, then carried her to the door and reluctantly woke her with soft kisses before setting her on her feet.

"Sweetheart, you're my last delivery. Get some rest." Ashton hoped she would call in and quit in the morning.

Chapter 17

Dominique knew she was in big trouble the next morning when she could hardly move. Of course, she didn't know that she was almost mummified until Ashton called to check on her.

"Sweetheart, are you sure you want to do this again?" he asked in a gentle tone. "I tried my best to take it easy on you, and that kind of slowed us down. Another driver would be all business."

She so much wanted to agree with him. At least her body was begging her to, but she wasn't a quitter. "I like to finish what I start."

"I'm all for this when it comes to us outside of work."

"I'll be ready at ten. Bye," She said in defiance, then dragging herself out the bed, she slid down the side until her knees hit the floor. With her face flat on the bed, she prayed to God for thanksgiving to see another day.

Before taking a shower, she checked her emails. Two jumped out at her: one from Mr. Jeffries. She opened that one first. She'd been copied on a letter to her direct boss, David. She couldn't believe he was making a fuss about her delivering packages. The next email was David's with Mr. Jeffries cc.

Dominique,

Mr. Jeffries contacted me, concerned and shocked to see a senior accounts manager moonlighting. As you are aware, it is against company policy for management to work a second job. You are advised to be on a conference call at 9:30 this morning to explain your actions.

David Sinks
Regional Director
Global Payroll Solutions

"What?" Dominique couldn't believe what she was reading. Were they serious? "Lord, help me. I can't lose my six-figure salary over this." Checking the time, she had fifteen minutes until the conference call and forty-five minutes before Ashton arrived. What if she hadn't checked her email? Thank God she did.

On a typical day, Dominique had her prep time before leaving the house down to a science, usually one hour and twenty minutes. Not this day. There was no telling what she would look like.

After setting the timer on her phone, Dominique winced as she moved to get in the shower. Seven minutes later, she was applying lotion, then minimal makeup. With a minute to spare, she joined the conference call.

After pressing in the code, she was advised there were four people on the call. Four? She announced herself, and David gave her a curt greeting, then got down to business. "Mr. Jeffries is on the call, as well as Juanita Peebles from HR and Lea Fields from PR. Now, Mr. Jeffries was disturbed seeing his top performing accounts manager dressed down, delivering boxes. You do know this is against company policy…" he rambled.

"Miss Hayes," Mr. Jeffries addressed her, "what if one of our clients had seen you in that getup doing manual labor? Image is everything, and ours is polished, so please explain why you shouldn't be fired immediately."

Dominique wanted to remind them that she was on her time, not the company's, but she doubted that would help her defense. *God, please guide my words.* "I apologize if my actions were anyway misunderstood. I took vacation days so my activities would not interfere with my job duties. I even check my emails for emergencies, which is how I learned about this last minute conference call." She hoped they got the hint. "Every year, my family and I perform community service for the holidays. The funds will be donated to a charity of my choice." Her heart pounded, hoping this would pacify upper management.

"She does have a point,"

Lea Fields, the company's public relations director,

said. "I could spin a press release on this, stating Global Payroll Solutions senior manager works for charity. Too bad we don't have pictures."

"I happened to take a selfie with the driver yesterday." Who knew she would need it to save her day job?

"Excellent," Lea said. "Please forward that to my email along with the driver's name."

How did something so simple and innocent get blown out of portion? "As a matter of fact, I signed up for two weeks. And the driver will be here..." She glanced over her shoulder at the time. "In twenty minutes."

"Dominique," Juanita Peebles, the human resources director, spoke for the first time. "Our company supports charity work, but please consult me or someone in my office the next time you want to do community service to make sure it is approved first."

When did community service become political? She wondered, but didn't voice.

"Well, take more pictures, especially with the boxes. Can you wear a Santa hat?" Lea jumped back in.

"No, I can't. I'm a Christian, and we celebrate Christ during Christmas."

"Never mind," Mr. Jeffries said. "Next time you decide to do a promo op, please work with David and Juanita for an approved angle. We're highly educated professionals, not hourly manual laborers."

How demeaning? Manual laborers added growth to the economy. Global Payroll Solutions courted companies which employed union workers alongside salaried staff. Dominique kept her peace, instead of reminding them of that. She had more respect for what Ashton did effortlessly.

"Dominique, it's a great thing you're doing, but I think one week is long enough for publicity purposes," Mr. Sinks, her direct manager, advised.

She had to agree with him on that one. She doubted her body could take that kind of punishment for two weeks anyway.

"And if you happen to run into one of our clients while delivering packages, please explain to them this is company-sponsored community service," Mr. Jeffries advised.

She wasn't about to lie. "Thank you for your understanding, but I must go."

Once she exited the conference, she praised and thanked God for giving her the words to say and regrouped before Ashton arrived, and he was on time.

"What's wrong?" was the first thing out of his mouth when she opened the door. "I can tell by looking into your eyes."

She waited until they boarded the truck, then gave him a recap of what had happened last night and that morning. She never had seen Ashton angry before.

"And they were going to fire you for taking a second job? Incredible." His nostrils flared. "They might own the company, but it was the workers who helped their companies grow." When they stopped at a red light, he reached over and embraced her. "I know you're doing this to be with me, but if you ever lose your job, I make enough to take care of you and a family without batting an eye." He grunted. "Nobody

127

messes with my baby!"

Dominique actually smiled. "You sound like my father."

Ashton released a hearty laugh. "I'll take that as a compliment."

Their stops were completely different that day. The most interesting client was at Nancy's Floral Pot.

The owner gave her a hug. "So you're the pretty thing who has been getting my flowers. God bless you child." She whispered, "Ashton is a good catch. Tighten the reel and don't let go."

Dominique wouldn't, not even for Global Payroll Solutions. Her skills, education, and experience were transferable to several careers. She doubted the Lord had created another Ashton, no matter how bad she wanted one for Paige.

Ashton was relieved when Dominique's company limited her time as a driver's helper, although he wasn't happy about her being forced to end it. Only because of her was he dressing in a suit and tie to mingle with the same bigwigs who threatened Dominique's job at the company Christmas party.

Since Paige wasn't available to go on a shopping spree with Dominique to purchase a dress for the soccasion, Ashton had tagged along. Although he wasn't a shopper, he enjoyed the experience of watching her try on dresses and look to him for his approval.

Of course, after the sixth shop and dress change, he would agree to anything, so they could leave. That was until she stepped out in a silver dress that hugged her curves. Ashton's mouth suddenly went dry, and he felt weak although he was sitting. The dress flared from her tiny waist and stopped above the knees, but there was a sheer fabric on top of the skirt that continued to her ankles. Yes, he liked.

He didn't have to say a word for her to know it. Ashton decided to purchase it as one of her Christmas presents. When he told her his intentions, it hadn't gone over well.

"Flowers and small gifts are acceptable. I didn't invite you to come and spend big money on me." She gave him a fierce look.

He leaned closer. "Number one, I'm not scared of you." He smirked and wiggled his brows. "Number two, unless you're my wife…you can't tell me how to spend my money on the woman I love. And speaking of a wife, we need to have some long talks without distractions." He returned to the counter and whipped out his credit card.

"That will be one-hundred sixty-three dollars and twelve cents, sir," the tall unnaturally red-haired woman said pleasantly. "You saved seventy-two dollars today."

Accepting his credit card back and the hanger with the garment wrapped in plastic, he tossed it over his shoulder with one hand, and he wrapped his other arm around her waist. "I told you when we first met, you can't break my bank. As a matter of fact, I earn enough to take care of a family of four or five," he shrugged, "or as many as the mother of my children wants." He smirked. "Now, are we ready to leave?"

Giggling, Dominique shook her head. "Nope. I've got to find shoes to match."

Nooooo. Keeping a straight face, he followed.

"And this time, I'm paying."

A few days later, as he prepped in the mirror, Ashton couldn't wait to see Dominique in her full ensemble. He was a blessed man.

Once he was donned in a three-piece gray pinstripe suit, he admired the bronzish color tie that Dominique had picked. At first glance, he thought it would clash. But a double take, showed him it worked.

After grabbing his keys and wallet, he draped his wool coat over his arm and strolled out of the house. He chuckled to himself. He had never been so dressed up, and he felt like a character out of a *Harlem Nights* movie.

Half hour later, he was standing outside Dominique's door. When she opened it, his heart thundered against his chest. She was nothing shy of a princess. All she needed was a crown. "Wow, I'm blessed to have you." He stepped inside and kissed her softly, then tamed his emotions.

Her eyes sparkled as she scanned his attire. He did a quick spin as if he was on a runway. "Did I clean up?"

"Real good." She took a deep breath and exhaled. "I'll get my wrap. We're going to the Tapawingo National Golf Club in Sunset Hills."

"I've already got the address programmed into my

GPS." After draping the cape over her shoulders, he hugged her, and rested his chin on her shoulder. "I love you, you know that?"

"Yes," she said softly and rubbed his beard without turning around. "Your love was worth every prayer I prayed for a mate." She turned in his arms." And they shared the sweetest hug before he took her hand and led her to his car.

During the forty-five-minute drive to South County, they commented on the Christmas lights they could see from I-270. Last Saturday, he had helped her string some up on her house. He didn't bother with his. With his work schedule, he wouldn't be at home to enjoy them, or even turn them on.

"Have you finished your Christmas shopping?" she asked.

"Yep. Gift cards, or cards with cash inside. Either way, it's easy."

She playfully slapped his shoulder. "That's so impersonal. What I didn't buy in the store, I ordered online."

He grunted. "Yes, I know. I delivered them, remember?" They laughed together. "One thing our pastor teaches us at Corinthian Church about Christmas is a fact that many people forget. The wise men who brought Jesus gifts, worshiped Him and Him alone, not Mary, not Joseph, but Jesus alone. There's very little gift giving to Jesus or worshiping Him this time of year."

Dominique nodded. "He's right. Amen."

"Yes, and Pastor Garmany reminds us each year as Apostolic Pentecostals, if we do decide to celebrate

Christmas and give gifts, to give Christ the biggest gift, not our parents, or children, or—"

"Girlfriend." She gasped, then faced him. "Did you go over budget with my gift—this dress I'm wearing? I'm sorry, if you weren't planning to give that much in an offering..."

"No, babe." He glanced at her, then refocused on the road. "My offering will be more than two hundred bucks, so I'm good, and there's no problem. Jesus will always be the center of my Christmas."

"Amen. I do Christian Christmas too, and I don't go overboard, but I like giving Christ the best gift."

"And this year—" he lifted her hand to his lips and kissed it—"Jesus gave me you. Hallelujah."

Dominique felt like royalty with her prince at her side as Ashton followed the winding road through the country club lit like a winter wonderland. The mansion sat on a hill that gave a great view of the golf club in the daytime.

Valets greeted them as Ashton handed over the keys and rounded the car to her. They walked up the steps to the entrance.

"This is beautiful." She was in awe.

Ashton agreed as he kept a hand on her back.

Once inside, she recognized most of the account executives. They checked their coats and began to mingle, declining the champagne offered by the waiters, since they didn't drink.

When she spotted her regional manager, she leaned into Ashton. "That's the big boss who accepted the delivery that night."

She felt Ashton's muscles flex as he turned to her with a scowl weighing down his face. "Should I have an attitude?"

"No. Everything turned out okay."

He grunted and seemed to relax as they steered clear of upper management, enjoying the hors d'oeuvres and Sprite or sparkling juice.

Dominique knew she couldn't avoid her bosses, so she said a short prayer and guided Ashton in their direction.

"Merry Christmas, Dominique!" Mr. Jeffries lifted his glass in a salute, and her direct boss, David Sinks, followed suit.

"Merry Christmas." She turned to Ashton, whose smile didn't reach his eyes. "This is my date, Ashton Taylor."

Nodding, Ashton shook hands with both of them. She counted to ten before one of them asked what he did for a living.

"I'm in logistics."

"Where?" Mr. Sinks asked.

"Package Express."

She and Ashton waited for realization to hit them.

"I thought you looked familiar. Dominique   sent us a picture." Then Mr. Jeffries snapped his finger. "Were you the driver that night Dominique delivered packages?"

"I am." He snaked his hand around her waist   and

nudged her closer to him. She felt cherished, and his gesture didn't go unnoticed by either man.

"I see. Well, enjoy yourself tonight." And after a curt nod, her managers dismissed themselves.

Ashton steered her to a random table for them to sit for dinner. He whispered in her ear, "I so wanted to thump my chest against his and ask if he had a problem with my chosen career."

Linking her fingers through his, she smiled to calm him down. "This is a spiritual battle. Blessed are the meek, for we shall inherit the earth. You're a good man, Ashton Taylor. We also know God wants us to conduct ourselves—"

"I know, babe. Silently strong, secretly wise beyond measure, and quietly powerful, so we aren't easily provoked." He leaned his forehead against hers and whispered, "I wouldn't trade you for anything in the world. You're truly a godly woman, and my soul-mate."

She loved hearing him say that.

"If I asked you to marry me tonight, would you?"

Dominique blinked back her surprise. She felt her mouth open, but no words came out. Finally, she could speak. "Do you have a ring tonight?"

He chuckled. "No, my princess."

"Then, no I wouldn't, my prince."

Ashton nodded and glanced around. "That's good to know."

Chapter 18

Ashton made a detour before he visited Dominique. Her message was loud and clear about an engagement ring, which he hadn't had time to shop for, clocking more than sixty-five hours this week alone.

He rang the bell at her parents' house. Mrs. Hayes greeted him at the door with a familiar smile like her daughter's, then a hug.

"It's so nice to see you again," Mrs. Hayes said and ushered him inside where Mr. Hayes was standing in the living room. The two shook hands.

"Have a seat, Ashton," he said, then took a seat, and Mrs. Hayes joined him.

What a contrast, Ashton thought as he looked from one to the other. Dora Hayes' eyes twinkled while Byron's expression was blank.

"Thank you for seeing me." Ashton cleared his throat as Dominique's mother leaned forward in anticipation while her husband sat back with folded arms. "I love your daughter…" Dora smiled. "And I want to marry her for life."

Byron's expression remained unimpressed. "I've had one wife and one daughter, and they are my sole priorities. I have loved them and protected them." He reached for Dora's hand, and she slid hers in his. A hint of a smile moved his lips. "I've been a provider and faithful. If you're not a forever type of man in your heart, then walk away now."

"Honey." Dora frowned at her husband.

He turned and gave her a tender look. "It's okay, hon. I can't sugarcoat this. Dominique is all we have." He faced Ashton again. "You see, I don't know how many weddings I've attended when the groom pledges his faithfulness, and before the clock strikes midnight, he's in the bed with a mistress or bridesmaid."

Ashton briefly thought about his coworker who couldn't remain faithful.

"God gave Eve to Adam. Have you prayed on this and feel God has given you Dominique?"

"Yes, sir." He patiently listened to her father's passionate monologue. After about twenty minutes or so, he received a text. Byron's eyebrow went up.

Ashton chuckled when he read the message. He wiped the smile off his mouth when he faced her father who didn't share his amusement. Ashton knew he didn't have to share what Dominique had written, but he wanted to prove to them, he had nothing to hide. He stood and showed them the message:

Will you stop and bring some more coloring books? Love u so much, D.

They laughed too. "It's a hobby we haven't shared in a long time, so, Mr. Hayes, is your answer a yes or no?"

Getting to his feet, Byron extended his hand. "It's a yes, but I will be watching you."

Ashton turned to Dora who was blinking back tears. "I will love her."

"I know," she whispered and sniffed before hugging him.

Exhaling, Ashton thanked them. "Now, if you'll excuse me, it's looks like I need to get those coloring books."

The day after Christmas, Dominique woke to someone ringing her doorbell. She peeked out the window to spy Ashton's truck. Fussing to herself, she hurried in her bathroom and washed her face, brushed her teeth and fluffed her hair. She had no scheduled deliveries, if Ashton couldn't wait for her to make herself presentable, then he could leave her package at the door.

Dominique patted her face with some moisture, adjusted her top, then went to open the door.

"Hey, baby." He greeted her with a kiss as his cold breath filled the chilly air with every word he spoke. "For you." He handed her a bouquet of at least a dozen roses, a jumbo chocolate cupcake with slices of strawberries on top, and a card.

He kissed her on the lips again. "Got to go. Make sure you read my card." Adjusting the cap on his head, he jogged back to his truck, waved, and drove away.

Closing the door, she stared at the flowers. What was he up to? Yesterday, he lavished her with several gifts like a music box, shawl, and other thoughtful gifts. They had talked more about marriage and she had hope one gift included a ring, but it didn't and she did her best to hide her disappointment.

In her kitchen, she used a familiar vase for his flowers, made her a cup of coffee to drink with the cake, then sat to open his card.

The best between us is yet to come. Say yes tonight, he scribbled, *Ashton.*

Tonight? The only plans they had made was to attend the singles meeting at her church. She called Paige who was off work, because of the holiday. "Hey, I just got a delivery from Ashton."

"Okay, so tell me something I don't know." Her friend chuckled.

Dominique read her the cryptic message. "What do you think he means?" She frowned. "Do you think he's going to propose?"

"It's about time," Paige said. "It's taken him long enough. He should have done it yesterday..." her friend rambled on without confirming Dominique's suspicion.

"We had planned to come to the singles meeting tonight."

Paige laughed. "Well, if you two don't show up, then I'll conclude he asked and you gave him the correct answer." She paused and released a sigh. "I am so happy for you. Once I've been on this job for a year, I'm going to move out of my parents' house for a second time, hopefully, for good. I guess I'll be opening my door well groomed, full makeup included."

"You're so silly." Dominique grinned as she re-read the card. "I have to admit I always played out the moment of my proposal. Somewhere romantic, private, and a complete surprise. I have to say, even with the heads up, I didn't see this coming. Yesterday, I kind of hoped for it, but the day after Christmas, it is a surprise."

"Well, I'll let you go so you can get ready for your big night. Pre-congrats and I'm happy and love you."

"Love you more." They disconnected, and Dominique decided she needed something new to wear, so within the hour, she was at the Galleria.

Chapter 19

All day, Ashton couldn't keep his mind off of his proposal. Although he was secure in their love, he was nervous. He had heard horror stories about men proposing and the women leaving them hanging, which was why he wanted a more private setting.

If he was going to get wounded, he didn't want anyone to see. Ashton second guessed himself on Christmas Day when he saw the flash of disappointment on Dominique's face when a ring wasn't among her gifts from him. He started to pull out the ring then, but decided against it. Even her father's raised brow didn't sway him.

His coworker, Marc, thought Ashton was joking when they reported to the hub that morning. "So, you're really going to do it? Get married?"

"Yep." Ashton grinned and rocked on his heels. He was feeling pretty good today. Christmas was over, but he was just as excited as a child about to get their Christmas wish. "If Dominique follows my instructions and says yes, I'll be an engaged man."

"What a minute." Marc released a whoop, and the more he tried to stop, the more he barked out his amusement. "Let…let me get this right. You *told* Dominique to marry you?" Ashton nodded with a shrug and his friend snickered. "Maybe that's where I went wrong, I asked." Trying to suppress more laughter, Marc gulped for air. "Don't come back in here whining, because she hurt your feelings and said no."

"I have no shame in pursuing what I want, and I want Dominique as my wife." He grinned and winked. "And my woman knows it. Tonight, so don't ask for any favors. Once I finish my load, I'm out of here!"

Marc made a ridiculous gesture of bowing as he backed away. "Dare I come between your romantic proposal." When they parted ways, his coworker was still laughing.

It was about eleven when Ashton decided to break for lunch and call Dominique. "Hey, baby."

"Hi." Did her voice sound seductive or was it just him? "The flowers are beautiful and the cupcake was scrumptious," she said.

Ashton smirked. She was toying with him. "And the card? Have you been practicing your answer?" he teased.

"I hope you have practiced your lines." She giggled and he loved the sound of her being happy.

141

"You can grade me tonight. Love you," he whispered and waited for her to return his affections. She did, then he blew her a kiss and got back to his deliveries. No way would Ashton keep his lady waiting. Not tonight, and his determination was the source of him leaving work on time.

At home, Ashton donned another suit, only for Dominique would he get this overdressed. After double checking his appearance, he patted the ring box in his pocket. Half hour later, he rang Dominique's bell and waited. When she opened the door, her face glowed with happiness. She wore red—adding to the list of his favorite colors—which set his heart on fire. His nostrils flared. He prayed she wouldn't keep him waiting long to tie the knot. "Ready?"

"The answer is yes."

Laughing, Ashton lifted her off the floor. "Baby, you're supposed to wait for the proposal." He lowered her and kissed her lips. "At least let me recite what I practiced."

She giggled. "Okay. I'll be good."

He doubted that as he helped Dominique into her coat to leave. Once in the car, they both seemed to be tortured by the silence when their pending engagement was about to make both of them explode.

It was amusing and a couple of times, they glanced at each other and laughed. Reaching for her hand, he kissed it. "I love you, Sister Hayes."

"Not for long—oops, I'm not supposed to say that am I?" She grinned then turned to look out the window, giggling.

His heart swelled with happiness. Tonight was all

about mesmerizing his future wife. Their reservations were at Kemoll's Italian Restaurant at the top of the Metropolitan Square building. The view overlooking downtown, the Mississippi River, and the Gateway Arch was breathtaking.

Once they parked underground, they rode the two elevators needed to get to the top floor. Dominique became quiet. Ashton hoped she wasn't having second thoughts.

He leaned in and whispered, "Did I tell you how stunning you look tonight?"

"You can always tell me again." She batted her eyes right before the elevator doors opened. Since the holidays were over, the restaurant wasn't crowded as he had hoped for a more intimate setting. With his arm secure around her small waist, they followed the hostess to their table.

Their server attended to them immediately and took their orders. Left alone, Ashton reached for Dominique's hands, and noticed they were trembling. They both were nervous. He wouldn't torture her for much longer. Leaning across the table, he brushed his lips against hers. "I've been waiting all my life for you."

"I've been waiting all day for you." She pouted. "I prayed that you wouldn't be late."

He shook his head. "Peak season is done. This— you—were too important for me to chance working one hour over."

Their salads arrived, and Ashton bowed his head and gave thanks for their food. But after a few bites, he rested his fork. Although he was starving,   Ashton couldn't eat. "Sweetheart, am I what you want? Everything you had hoped for in a God-fearing man? I don't want to disappoint you in any way."

"You're a trendsetter when it comes to love. My disappointment about your job interfering with our dates in the beginning was unfounded after being your driver's helper." She chuckled. "That's hard work and I respect you for that."

"Thank you, baby, but I'll never make a date I can't keep."

"Bringing me flowers and lunch, and suggesting we rake my yard together. It's those little things that are special to me," she said slowly, "biting your tongue when my bosses tried to belittle you is a big deal. You're amazing." Her eyes sparkled with unshed tears, but if one dropped, he would catch it.

She blushed. "I was hoping and praying for a proposal yesterday on Christmas."

"Nah, that's too cliché." He scrunched his nose playfully and shook his head.

"Well, giving me a heads up was definitely different, but changed it. You definitely made my day."

"That's good to know why you love me."

Their server arrived with their stuffed baked chicken and roasted vegetables, but paused when he saw their salads were barely touched. Ashton looked to Dominique. She nodded for the server to take away her salad. "I'm too nervous to eat." She glanced out the window. "The view is breathtaking."

"And so are you. I chose this place because the day I saw you, I felt lifted off the ground, and you've

144

had my head in the clouds ever since. Now, the reason I love you is because you love God. I can imagine it's been hard to fight off every successful man who wanted to win your heart, but you waited." He choked. "For me, for God to send me."

"Is this part of the rehearsed proposal?"

"Yes, the beginning." Standing, he held his hand and guided Dominique to her feet, then led her to a sitting area away from the other diners. Once she was comfortable on a velvet bench, he knelt. Her tears began to fall. Using his thumb, he gently wiped at them.

"Dominique Joyce Hayes, you made me ready to be a husband the day I found a virtuous woman, then I knew I was complete spiritually. The Bible says, two are better than one. People say, the woman is the better half. I say, you make me a better man. I've waited long enough to be loved by the perfect woman, so tonight…" He paused and pulled out the ring box, then flipped it open and took the ring out. "The double band fused reminds me of us together, holding up a valuable treasure. Of course, the diamond symbolizes our love." He teased the tip of her finger with it. "Will you marry me for life?"

"Yes, for life." She nodded as he slid the ring all the way on.

Standing, Dominique encircled his neck. Her eyes were glazed over, reflecting her love. "I can shout, Hallelujah, Lord. Thanks for my special delivery." She sealed it with a kiss.

Book Club Discussion

1. Did Dominique had a legitimate complaint about Ashton's work schedule and dates? Why or why not?

2. Discuss Dominique's boss's reaction to her delivering packages.

3. Dominique made a vow to God to date practicing Christian men. Discuss her decision. Does it matter?

4. What did you think of Ashton giving Dominique a hint of his upcoming proposal?

5. What message did this story have for Christian singles?

***I hope you had fun reading Ashton and Dominique's story. Please consider posting a quick review on Amazon or Goodreads, and visiting patsimmons.net and joining my newsletter for updates about my books, tour, and family.

About the Author

Pat is celebrating ten years as a multi-published author of more than thirty Christian titles, and is a three-time recipient of the Emma Rodgers Award for Best Inspirational Romance. She has been a featured speaker and workshop presenter at various venues across the country.

As a self-proclaimed genealogy sleuth, Pat is passionate about researching her ancestors and then casting them in starring roles in her novels. She describes the evidence of the gift of the Holy Ghost as an amazing, unforgettable, life-altering experience. God is the Author who advances the stories she writes. Pat currently oversees the media publicity for the annual RT Booklovers Conventions. She has a B.S. in mass communications from Emerson College in Boston, Massachusetts.

Pat converted her sofa-strapped, sports fanatic husband into an amateur travel agent, untrained bodyguard, GPS-guided chauffeur, and administrative assistant who is constantly on probation. They have a son and a daughter.

Other Christian titles include:

The Guilty series
Book I: *Guilty of Love*
Book II: *Not Guilty of Love*
Book III: *Still Guilty*
Book IV: *The Acquittal*

The Jamieson Legacy
Book I: *Guilty by Association*
Book II: *The Guilt Trip*
Book III: *Free from Guilt*
Book IV: *The Confession*

The Carmen Sisters
Book I: *No Easy Catch*
Book II: *In Defense of Love*
Book III: *Driven to Be Loved*
Book IV: *Redeeming Heart*

Love at the Crossroads
Book I: *Stopping Traffic*
Book II: *A Baby for Christmas*
Book III: *The Keepsake*
Book IV: *What God Has for Me*
Book V: *Every Woman Needs A Praying Man*

Making Love Work Anthology
Book I: *Love at Work*
Book II: *Words of Love*

Book III: *A Mother's Love*

Restore My Soul series
Crowning Glory
Jet: The Back Story
Love Led by the Spirit

Single titles
Talk to Me
Her Dress (novella)
Christmas Greetings
Couple by Christmas
Love By Delivery

Anderson Brothers
Book I: Three novellas: *A Christian Christmas, A Christian Easter, and*
A Christian Father's Day
Book II: *A Woman After David's Heart (Valentine's Day)*
Book III: *A Noelle for Nathan* (Book 3 of the Andersen Brothers)

Restore My Soul series

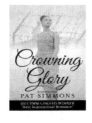

Crowning Glory, Book 1. Cinderella had a prince; Karyn Wallace has a King. While Karyn served four years in prison for an unthinkable crime, she embraced salvation through Crowns for Christ outreach ministry. After her release, Karyn stays strong and confident, despite the stigma society places on ex-offenders. Since Christ strengthens the underdog, Karyn refuses to sway away from the scripture, "He who the Son has set free is free indeed." Levi Tolliver, for the most part, is a practicing Christian. One contradiction is he doesn't believe in turning the other cheek. He's steadfast there is a price to pay for every sin committed, especially after the untimely death of his wife during a robbery. Then Karyn enters Levi's life. He is enthralled not only with her beauty, but her sweet spirit until he learns about her incarceration. If Levi can accept that Christ paid Karyn's debt in full, then a treasure awaits him. This is a powerful tale and reminds readers of the permanency of redemption.

Jet: The Back Story to Love Led By the Spirit, Book 2.
To say Jesetta "Jet" Hutchens has issues is an understatement. In *Crowning Glory*, Book 1 of the Restoring My Soul

series, she releases a firestorm of anger with an unforgiving heart. But every hurting soul has a history. In *Jet: The Back Story to Love Led by the Spirit,* Jet doesn't know how to cope with the loss of her younger sister, Diane.

But God sets her on the road to a spiritual recovery. To make sure she doesn't get lost, Jesus sends the handsome and single Minister Rossi Tolliver to be her guide.

Psalm 147:3 says Jesus can heal the brokenhearted and bind up their wounds. That sets the stage for *Love Led by the Spirit.*

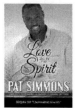

Love Led By the Spirit, Book 3. Minister Rossi Tolliver is ready to settle down. Besides the outwardly attraction, he desires a woman who is sweet, humble, and loves church folks. Sounds simple enough on paper, but when he gets off his knees, praying for that special someone to come into his life, God opens his eyes to the woman who has been there all along. There is only a slight problem. Love is the farthest thing from Jesetta "Jet" Hutchens' mind. But Rossi, the man and the minister, is hard to resist. Is Jet ready to allow the Holy Spirit to lead her to love?

Love at the Crossroads Series

Stopping Traffic, Book 1. Candace Clark has a phobia about crossing the street, and for good reason.

As fate would have it, her daughter's principal assigns her to crossing guard duties as part of the school's Parent Participation program. With no choice in the matter, Candace begrudgingly accepts her stop sign and safety vest, then reports to her designated crosswalk. Once Candace is determined to overcome her fears, God opens the door for a blessing, and Royce Kavanaugh enters into her life, a firefighter built to rescue any damsel in distress. When a spark of attraction ignites, Candace and Royce soon discover there's more than one way to stop traffic.

A Baby For Christmas, Book 2. Yes, diamonds are a girl's best friend, but in Solae Wyatt-Palmer's case, she desires something more valuable. Captain Hershel Kavanaugh is a divorcee and the father of two adorable little boys. Solae has never been married and longs to be a mother. Although Hershel showers her with expensive gifts, his hesitation about proposing causes Solae to walk and never look back. As the holidays approach, Hershel must convince Solae that she has everything he could ever want for Christmas.

The Keepsake, Book 3. Until death us do part...or until Desiree walks away. Desiree "Desi" Bishop is devastated when she finds evidence of her husband's affair. God knew she didn't get married only to one day have to stand before a judge and file for a divorce. But Desi wants out no matter how much her heart says to forgive Michael. That isn't easier said than done. She sees God's one acceptable reason for a divorce as the only opt-out clause in her marriage. Michael Bishop is a repenting man who loves his wife of three years. If only...he had paid attention to the red flags God sent to keep him from falling into the devil's snares. But Michael didn't and he had fallen. Although God had forgiven him instantly when he repented, Desi's forgiveness is moving as a snail's pace. In the end, after all the tears have been shed and forgiveness granted and received, the couple learns that some marriages are worth keeping

What God Has For Me, Book 4. Halcyon Holland is leaving her live-in boyfriend, taking their daughter and the baby in her belly with her. She's tired of waiting for the ring, so she buys herself one.

When her ex doesn't reconcile their relationship, Halcyon begins to second-guess whether or not she compromised her chance for a happily ever after. After all, what man in his right mind would want to deal with the community stigma of 'baby mama drama?' But Zachary Bishop has had his eye on Halcyon since the first time he saw her. Without a ring on her finger, Zachary prays that she will come to her senses and not only leave Scott, but come back to God. What one man doesn't cherish, Zach is ready to treasure. Not deterred by Halcyon's broken spirit, Zachary is on a mission to offer her a second chance at love that she can't refuse. And as far as her adorable children are concerned, Zachary's love is unconditional for a ready-made family. Halcyon will soon learn that her past circumstances won't hinder the Lord's blessings, because what God has for her, is for her…and him…and the children.

Every Woman Needs A Praying Man, Book 5. First impressions can make or break a business deal and they definitely could be a relationship buster, but an ill-timed panic attack draws two strangers together. Unlike firefighters who run into danger, instincts tell businessman Tyson Graham to head the other way as fast as he can when he meets a certain damsel in distress. Days later, the same woman struts through his door for a job interview. Monica Wyatt might possess the outwardly beauty and the brains on paper, but Tyson doesn't trust her to work for his firm, or maybe he doesn't trust his heart around her.

The Andersen Brothers Holiday Series

 *A* leave, disappointing her and the children. Although Christian Christmas. Christian's Christmas will never be the same for Joy Knight if Christian Andersen has his way. Not to be confused with a secret Santa, Christian and his family are busier than Santa's elves making sure the Lord's blessings are distributed to those less fortunate by Christmas day. Joy is playing the hand that life dealt her, rearing four children in a home that is on the brink of foreclosure. She's not looking for a handout, but when Christian rescues her in the checkout line; her niece thinks Christian is an angel. Joy thinks he's just another man who will eventually Christian is a servant of the Lord, he is a flesh and blood man and all he wants for Christmas is Joy Knight. Can time spent with Christian turn Joy's attention from her financial woes to the real meaning of Christmas—and true love?

 *A Christian Easter.*, How to celebrate Easter becomes a balancing act for Christian and Joy Andersen and their four children. Chocolate bunnies, colorful stuffed baskets and flashy fashion shows are their competition. Despite the enticements, Christian refuses to succumb without a

fight. And it becomes a tug of war when his recently adopted ten year-old daughter, Bethani, wants to participate in her friend's Easter tradition. Christian hopes he has instilled Proverbs 22:6, into the children's heart in the short time of being their dad.

A Christian Father's Day. Three fathers, one Father's Day and four children. Will the real dad, please stand up. It's never too late to be a father—or is it? Christian Andersen was looking forward to spending his first Father's day with his adopted children---all four of them. But Father's day becomes more complicated than Christian or Joy ever imagined. Christian finds himself faced with living up to his name when things don't go his way to enjoy an idyllic once a year celebration. But he depends on God to guide him through the journey.

A Woman After David's Heart, Book 2, David Andersen doesn't have a problem indulging in Valentine's Day, per se, but not on a first date. Considering it was the love fest of the year, he didn't want a woman to get any ideas that a wedding ring was forthcoming before he got a chance to know her. So he has no choice but to wait until the whole Valentine's Day hoopla was over, then he would make his move on a sister in his church he can't take his eyes off of. For the past two years and counting, Valerie Hart hasn't been the recipient of a romantic Valentine's Day dinner invitation. To fill the void, Valerie keeps herself busy with God's business, hoping the Lord will send her perfect mate soon. Unfortunately, with no prospects in sight, it looks like that won't happen again this year. A Woman After David's Heart is a Valentine romance novella that can be enjoyed with or without a box of chocolates.

A Noelle For Nathan, Book 3, is a story of kindness, selflessness, and falling in love during the Christmas season.

Andersen Investors & Consultants, LLC, CFO Nathan Andersen (A Christian Christmas) isn't looking for attention when he buys a homeless man a meal, but grade school teacher Noelle Foster is watching his every move with admiration. His generosity makes him a man after her own heart. While donors give more to children and families in need around the holiday season, Noelle Foster believes in giving year-round after seeing many of her students struggle with hunger and finding a warm bed at night. At a second-chance meeting, sparks fly when Noelle and Nathan share a kindred spirit with their passion to help those less fortunate. Whether they're doing charity work or attending Christmas parties, the couple becomes inseparable. Although Noelle and Nathan exchange gifts, the biggest present is the one from Christ.

Making Love Work Series

A Mother's Love. To Jillian Carter, it's bad when her own daughter beats her to the altar. She became a teenage mother when she confused love for lust one summer. Despite the sins of her past, Jesus forgave her and blessed her to be the best Christian example for Shana. Jillian is not looking forward to becoming an empty-nester at thirty-nine. The old adage, she's not losing a daughter, but gaining a son-in-law is not comforting as she braces for a lonely life ahead. What she doesn't expect is for two men to vie for her affections: Shana's biological father who breezes back into their lives as a redeemed man and practicing Christian. Not only is Alex still goof looking, but he's willing to right the wrong he's done in the past. Not if Dr. Dexter Harris has anything to say about it. The widower father of the groom has set his sights on Jillian and he's willing to pull out all the stops to woo her. Now the choice is hers. Who will be the next mother's love?

Love At Work. How do two people go undercover to hide an office romance in a busy television newsroom? In plain sight, of course. Desiree King is an assignment editor at KDPX-TV in St. Louis, MO. She dispatches a team to wherever breaking news happens. Her focus is to stay ahead of the competition. Overall, she's easy-going, respectable, and compassionate. But when it comes to dating a fellow coworker, she refuses to cross that professional line. Award-winning investigative reporter Bryan Mitchell makes life challenging for Desiree with his thoughtful gestures, sweet notes, and support. He tries to convince Desiree that as Christians, they could show coworkers how to blend their personal and private lives without compromising their morals.

Words Of Love. Call it old fashion, but Simone French was smitten with a love letter. Not a text, email, or Facebook post, but a love letter sent through snail mail. The prose wasn't the corny roses-are-red-and-violets-are-blue stuff. The first letter contained short accolades for a job well done. Soon after, the missives were filled with passionate words from a man who confessed the hidden secrets of his soul. He revealed his unspoken weaknesses, listed his uncompromising desires, and unapologetically noted his subtle strengths. Yes, Rice Taylor was ready to surrender to love. Whew. Closing her eyes, Simone inhaled the faint lingering smell of roses on the beige plain stationery. She had a testimony. If anyone would listen, she would proclaim that love was truly blind.

Single Titles

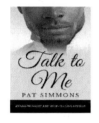

Talk To Me. Despite being deaf as a result of a fireworks explosion, CEO of a St. Louis non-profit company, Noel Richardson, expertly navigates the hearing world. What some view as a disability, Noel views as a challenge— his lack of hearing has never held him back. It also helps that he has great looks, numerous university degrees, and full bank accounts. But those assets don't define him as a man who longs for the right woman in his life. Deciding to visit a church service, Noel is blind-sided by the most beautiful and graceful Deaf interpreter he's ever seen. Mackenzie Norton challenges him on every level through words and signing, but as their love grows, their faith is tested. When their church holds a yearly revival, they witness the healing power of God in others. Mackenzie has faith to believe that Noel can also get in on the blessing. Since faith comes by hearing, whose voice does Noel hear in his heart, Mackenzie or God's?

TESTIMONY: If I Should Die Before I Wake. It is of the LORD's mercies that we are not consumed, because His compassions fail not. They are new every morning, great is Thy faithfulness.

Lamentations 3:22-23, God's mercies are sure; His promises are fulfilled; but a dawn of a new morning is God' grace. If you need a testimony about God's grace, then If I Should Die Before I Wake will encourage your soul. Nothing happens in our lives by chance. If you need a miracle, God's got that too. Trust Him. Has it been a while since you've had a testimony? Increase your prayer life, build your faith and walk in victory because without a test, there is no testimony. (ebook only)

Her Dress. Sometimes a woman just wants to splurge on something new, especially when she's about to attend an event with movers and shakers. Find out what happens when Pepper Trudeau is all dressed up and goes to the ball, but another woman is modeling the same attire.

At first, Pepper is embarrassed, then the night gets interesting when she meets Drake Logan. Her Dress is a romantic novella about the all too common occurrence—two women shopping at the same place. Maybe having the same taste isn't all bad. Sometimes a good dress is all you need to meet the man of your dreams. (ebook only)

Saige Carter loves everything about Christmas: the shopping, the food, the lights, and of course, Christmas wouldn't be complete without family and friends to share in the traditions they've created together. Plus, Saige is extra excited about her line of Christmas greeting cards hitting store shelves, but when she gets devastating news around the holidays, she wonders if she'll ever look at Christmas the same again. Daniel Washington is no Scrooge, but he'd rather skip the holidays altogether than spend them with his estranged family. After one too many arguments around the dinner table one year, Daniel had enough and walked away from the drama. As one year has turned into many, no one seems willing to take the first step toward reconciliation. When Daniel reads one of Saige's greeting cards, he's unsure if the words inside are enough to erase the pain and bring about forgiveness. Once God reveals to them His purpose for their lives, they will have a reason to rejoice.

Holidays haven't been the same for Derek Washington since his divorce. He and his ex-wife, Robyn, go out the way to avoid each other. This Christmas may be different when he decides to gives his son, Tyler, the family he once had before the split. Derek's going to need the Lord's intervention to soften his ex-wife's heart to agree. God's help doesn't come in the way he expected, but it's all good, because everything falls in place for them to be a couple by Christmas.

Senior Accounts Manager Dominique Hayes has it all money, a car and a condo. Well, almost. She's starting to believe love has passed her by. One thing for sure, she can't hurry God, so she continues to wait while losing hope that a special Godly man will ever make his appearance. Package Courier Ashton Taylor knows a man who finds a wife finds a good thing. The only thing standing in his way of finding the right woman is his long work hours. Or maybe not. A chance meeting changes everything. When love finally comes knocking, will Dominique open the door and accept Ashton's special delivery?

The Guilty Series Kick Off

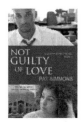

Guilty of Love. When do you know the most important decision of your life is the right one? Reaping the seeds from what she's sown; Cheney Reynolds moves into a historic neighborhood in Ferguson, Missouri, and becomes a reclusive. Her first neighbor, the incomparable Mrs. Beatrice Tilley Beacon aka Grandma BB, is an opinionated childless widow. Grandma BB is a self-proclaimed expert on topics Cheney isn't seeking advice—everything from landscaping to hip-hop dancing to romance. Then there is Parke Kokumuo Jamison VI, a direct descendant of a royal African tribe. He learned his family ancestry, African history, and lineage preservation before he could count. Unwittingly, they are drawn to each other, but it takes Christ to weave their lives into a spiritual bliss while He exonerates their past indiscretions.

Not Guilty. One man, one woman, one God and one big problem. Malcolm Jamieson wasn't the man who got away, but the man God instructed Hallison Dinkins to set free. Instead of their explosive love affair leading them to the wedding altar, God diverted Hallison to the prayer altar during her first visit back to church in years. Malcolm was convinced that his woman had loss her mind to break off their engagement. Didn't Hallison know that Malcolm, a tenth generation descendant of a royal African tribe, couldn't be replaced? Once Malcolm concedes that their relationship can't be savaged, he issues Hallison his own edict, "If we're meant to be with each other, we'll find our way back. If not, that means that there's a love stronger than what we had." His words begin to haunt Hallison until she begins to regret their break up, and that's where their story begins. Someone has to retreat, and God never loses a battle.

 *Still Guilty*. Cheney Reynolds Jamieson made a choice years ago that is now shaping her future and the future of the men she loves. A botched abortion left her unable to carry a baby to term, and her husband, Parke K. Jamison VI, is expected to produce heirs. With a wife who cannot give him a child, Parke vows to find and get custody of his illegitimate son by any means necessary. Meanwhile, Cheney's twin brother, Rainey, struggles with his anger over his ex-girlfriend's actions that haunt him, and their father, Dr. Roland Reynolds, fights to keep an old secret in the past.

 The Acquittal. Two worlds apart, but their hearts dance to the same African drum beat. On a professional level, Dr. Rainey Reynolds is a competent, highly sought-after orthodontist. Inwardly, he needs to be set free from the chaos of revelations that make him question if happiness is obtainable. To get away from the drama, Rainey is willing to leave the country under the guise of a mission trip with Dentist Without Borders. Will changing his surroundings really change him? If one woman can heal his wounds, then he will believe that there is really peace after the storm.

Ghanaian beauty Josephine Abena Yaa Amoah returns to Africa after completing her studies as an exchange student in St. Louis, Missouri. Although her heart bleeds for his peace, she knows she must step back and pray for Rainey's surrender to Christ in order for God to acquit him of his self-inflicted mental torture. In the Motherland of Ghana, Africa, Rainey not only visits the places of his ancestors, will he embrace the liberty that Christ's Blood really does set every man free.

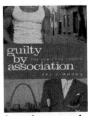 *Guilty By Association.* How important is a name? To the St. Louis Jamiesons who are tenth generation descendants of a royal African tribe—everything. To the Boston Jamiesons whose father never married their mother—there is no loyalty or legacy. Kidd Jamieson suffers from the "angry" male syndrome because his father was an absent in the home, but insisted his two sons carry his last name. It takes an old woman who mingles genealogy truths and Bible verses together for Kidd to realize his worth as a strong black man. He learns it's not his association with the name that identifies   him,

but the man he becomes that defines him.

The Guilt Trip. Aaron "Ace" Jamieson is living a carefree life. He's good-looking, respectable when he's in the mood, but his weakness is women. If a woman tries to ambush him with a pregnancy, he takes off in the other direction. It's a lesson learned from his absentee father that responsibility is optional. Talise Rogers has a bright future ahead of her. She's pretty and has no problem catching a man's eye, which is exactly what she does with Ace. Trapping Ace Jamieson is the furthest thing from Taleigh's mind when she learns she pregnant and Ace rejects her. "I want nothing from you Ace, not even your name." And Talise meant it.

Free From Guilt. It's salvation round-up time and Cameron Jamieson's name is on God's hit list. Although his brothers and cousins embraced God—thanks to the women in their lives—the two-degreed MIT graduate isn't going to let any woman take him down that path without a fight. He's satisfied with his career, social calendar, and good genes. But God uses a beautiful messenger, Gabrielle Dupree, to show him that he's in a spiritual deficit. Cameron learns the hard way that man's wisdom is like foolishness to God.

For every philosophical argument he throws her way, Gabrielle exposes him to scriptures that makes him question his worldly knowledge.

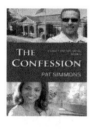

The Confession. Sandra Nicholson had made good and bad choices throughout the years, but the best one was to give her life to Christ when her sons were small and to rear them up in the best Christian way she knew how. That was thirty something years ago and Sandra has evolved from a young single mother of two rambunctious boys, Kidd and Ace Jamieson, to a godly woman seasoned with wisdom. Despite the challenges and trials of rearing two strong-willed personalities, Sandra maintained her sanity through the grace of God, which kept gray strands at bay. Now, Sandra Nicholson is on the threshold of happiness, but Kidd believes no man is good enough for his mother, especially if her love interest could be a man just like his absentee father.

The Carmen Sisters Series

No Easy Catch. Shae Carmen hasn't lost her faith in God, only the men she's come across. Shae's recent heartbreak was discovering that her boyfriend was not only married, but on the verge of reconciling with his estranged wife. Humiliated, Shae begins to second guess herself as why she didn't see the signs that he was nothing more than a devil's decoy masquerading as a devout Christian man. St. Louis Outfielder Rahn Maxwell finds himself a victim of an attempted carjacking. The Lord guides him out of harms' way by opening the gunmen's eyes to Rahn's identity. The crook instead becomes infatuated fan and asks for Rahn's autograph, and as a good will gesture, directs Rahn out of the ambush! When the news media gets wind of what happened with the baseball player, Shae's television station lands an exclusive interview. Shae and Rahn's chance meeting sets in motion a relationship where Rahn not only surrenders to Christ, but pursues Shae with a purpose to prove that good men are still out there. After letting her guard down, Shae is faced with another scandal that rocks her world. This time the stakes are higher. Not only is her heart on the line, so is her professional credibility. She and Rahn are at odds as how to handle it and friction erupts between them. Will she strike out at love again? The Lord shows Rahn that nothing happens by chance, and everything is done for Him to get the glory.

In Defense of Love. Lately, nothing in Garrett Nash's life has made sense. When two people close to the U.S. Marshal wrong him deeply, Garrett expects God to remove them from his life. Instead, the Lord relocates Garrett to another city to start over, as if he were the offender instead of the victim.

Criminal attorney Shari Carmen is comfortable in her own skin—most of the time. Being a "dark and lovely" African-American sister has its challenges, especially when it comes to relationships. Although she's a fireball in the courtroom, she knows how to fade into the background and keep the proverbial spotlight off her personal life. But literal spotlights are a different matter altogether. While playing tenor saxophone at an anniversary party, she grabs the attention of Garrett Nash. And as God draws them closer together, He makes another request of Garrett, one to which it will prove far more difficult to say "Yes, Lord."

Redeeming Heart. Landon Thomas (In Defense of Love) brings a new definition to the word "prodigal," as in prodigal son, brother or anything else imaginable. It's a good thing that God's love covers a multitude of sins, but He isn't letting Landon off easy. His journey from riches to rags proves to be humbling and a lesson well learned. Real Estate Agent Octavia Winston is a woman on a mission, whether it's God's or hers professionally. One thing is for certain, she's not about to compromise when it comes to a Christian mate, so why did God send a homeless man to steal her heart? Minister Rossi Tolliver (Crowning Glory) knows how to minister to God's lost sheep and through God's redemption, the game changes for Landon and Octavia.

Driven to Be Loved. On the surface, Brecee Carmen has nothing in common with Adrian Cole. She is a pediatrician certified in trauma care; he is a transportation problem solver for a luxury car dealership (a.k.a., a car salesman). Despite their slow but steady attraction to each other, neither one of them are sure that they're compatible. To complicate matters, Brecee is the sole unattached Carmen when it seems as though everyone else around her—family and friends—are finding love, except her.

Through a series of discoveries, Adrian and Brecee learn that things don't happen by coincidence. Generational forces are at work, keeping promises, protecting family members, and perhaps even drawing Adrian back to the church. For Brecee and Adrian, God has been hard at work, playing matchmaker all along the way for their paths cross at the right time and the right place.

Check out my fellow Christian fiction authors writing about faith, family, and love. You won't be disappointed!

www.blackchristianreads.com

Made in the USA
San Bernardino, CA
13 April 2017